I0557284

THE BLUES PLAY
HERBIE WATSON

James Flynn

Annadale Press

Annadale Press
London SW17 9TR

ISBN 0992783828
ISBN 978-0-9927838-2-2

For Stephanie

CHAPTER 1
A BIG DRAW

Herbie Watson put down his guitar case and sighed, his once handsome face set in chiseled downward lines, like a rock with indigestion. It was the usual upstairs room in a pub with a small bar in the corner and chairs and tables distributed in casual disarray. An oppressive silence emphasized the early evening gloom.

He looked at his watch, six o'clock, the organizers would not arrive before seven. There was no P.A. so all he had to do was tune up and hang around for an hour.

He took his guitar out of its case and sat down. His fingers rippled expertly over the strings. Finger picking classics from thirty years ago trooped from the sound hole in ritualistic progression: Candy man, Angi, Blues Run the Game, Guitar Shuffle and San Francisco Bay Blues. These songs had been the keys to his highway, will o' the wisps who had led him out over the slippery holes of life's no man's land, holding out the promise of a reality forever beyond his reach. He stopped playing and, placing his old Gibson J45 lovingly back in its case, went down stairs.

The pub was empty apart from one customer talking to a barman who served Herbie without interrupting the flow of their conversation. Herbie took his beer over to the farthest corner and sat down to wait. He was nursing his second pint when the organizers charged in.

There were two of them, Fred, a gaunt man with a wispy beard, tight lips and glasses, and his wife, Hettie, a large, fair haired, slow moving woman of uncertain age. They were carrying a cash box, a roll of tickets, a roll of raffle tickets and some leaflets. Nodding to the barman without stopping to buy a drink, they made their way upstairs. Herbie picked up his pint and followed after them.

By the time he got to the room he had managed to rake up a shop worn grin, but still no one acknowledged him, they were too busy arranging the chairs and tables in some semblance of order. Finally, Fred turned and raised an eyebrow in greeting.

"'Lo, Herbie." A man determined to remain unmoved in the presence of a star.

"Hello, Fred, long time no see."

"Yeah, the club's been doing well. You should have been here last week, the place was wall to wall. Next week is Sam Drummand, he's a big draw these days. I'm really looking forward to that one."

"Sounds good. I've got a box of CDs with me."

"Give them to Hettie, she can put a few on the table by the door, as soon as we've set it up. We don't want to be caught by the early rush ha, ha, ha."

The early rush turned out to be one fan from the old days. A small dilapidated man with a hypnotic stare, interrupted at irregular intervals by a twitch. Herbie frowned thoughtfully. He was on a hundred and fifty against a percentage of seventy percent, at this rate it didn't look as if he would break into the percentage. The fan wandered over.

"I remember I first saw you with Colney Hatch at the 1970 Duckworth festival."

He stiffened, two solo albums before and five after and all anyone could talk about was his four painful years with that bunch of wasters.

"And that hit you had," a reminiscent smile accompanied the twitch and the stare, "what was it now? You know."

"It's 1994, a lot of beer has gone down the..."

"'Beneath her Bonnie Bonnet.' That's it. My mother used to love that one."

Herbie had written the song after a week reading Burns poems. It had become a hit when someone had used it for a shampoo commercial. Now it looked as if it would be carved on his tombstone. The fan started to hum the chorus:

"Her een were blue
And sparkled too,
Like the rose with dew upon it.
I'd gie the world
To kiss the curl
Beneath her bonnie bonnet."

"Excuse me," said Herbie, "I've got to go and tune up." He went over to his guitar and made a few token adjustments, then he replaced it in the case and walked out the door, down the stairs and out into the street.

It was a cool evening in early September, the air gentle and comforting. He took a deep breath and immediately felt the tension in his muscles easing away. While he was walking, he reached into his back pocket and pulled out a silver hip flask. Good old Navy Rum, consolation in defeat and the first spoils of war in victory. He took a healthy slug and pushed it back into his jeans, ignoring the stares from a group of children by the village war memorial.

He turned down a side street. Ahead of him he saw a pub sign and across the road from it a church. The pub beckoned, but when he got down to it he noticed that there was some kind of function going on in the church hall. On an impulse he went over.

Popping his head through the door, he was surprised to see about a hundred people standing around drinking tea, eating cakes and talking in subdued voices. There were sprays of flowers in every corner and children's drawings of tractors, sheep and sheaves of hay under happy smiling suns on the walls. What was going on? Who or what was the big draw? With an expert eye born of long practice he began to do a rapid head count. People on the move could be deceptive, he liked them sitting in rows all facing one way. No, he hadn't overestimated, there were more than a hundred and that didn't include the children.

He was about to withdraw when he became aware of someone standing in front of him. He looked down and saw a tiny woman of about sixty five in a floral print dress, wearing a straw hat with a garden of flowers on it. She was smiling up at him and proffering a cup of tea.

"Cheers," he said, taking the cup. "What's all this in aid of?"

'We have just had the Harvest Festival service," she replied, "and we always have a little gathering afterwards, everybody's welcome."

Herbie nodded abstractedly and took a sip of tea. What a waste of a crowd, he thought, if he had this lot at his gig, not only would he wipe the long suffering look off Fred's face, but he would break the percentage and go home with about £350 in his pocket. No use dreaming, they looked as if they would all be tucked up in bed with their cocoa by nine o'clock. He moved morosely over to the refreshments table to give his cup back and thank the old ladies for the tea.

Suddenly, there was a mild commotion at the front of the hall and he turned to see the vicar climbing on to the stage. He was wearing a cream jacket over his black shirt, dog collar and black trousers. His greying black hair was cut across his forehead in a fringe which aimed at youthfulness, but was made vaguely disreputable by his dark jowl and professionally cheerful manner. He looked like a racing tout who was, regretfully, now going straight.

"Ladies and Gentlemen. Please!" he intoned in a rich, currant cake voice.

Oh, oh, thought Herbie, the sting, time to slide out. He began to shuffle unobtrusively towards the door as the vicar started his speech.

"First, I would like to say what a pleasure it is to see you all here today, giving your support to one of the happiest festivals in the church calendar. A chance to get together and thank Our Lord for the benefits bestowed on us through the year. Next, I would like to thank the helpers for their sterling work in decorating the church and hall to their usual high standard and, of course, let us not forget the children who gave the wonderful drawings which we can see all around us. And now, to business."

A ripple of laughter.

"As you know, we have been raising money for the repair of the church tower and, although you have all been extremely generous, we are still two thousand pounds short. We hope to have the full amount by Christmas, but thanks to the generosity of Mr. Frank Twistle, the landlord of the Nag's Head over the road, we might get a little closer to it this evening."

He reached down and somebody handed him a magnum of champagne which he held triumphantly aloft.

Mr. Twistle has donated this magnum of top quality champagne towards the church tower fund and I am going to auction it now. Come on, ladies and gentlemen, it's for a good cause, who is going to make the first bid?"

Herbie, who had almost reached the door, froze in his tracks. He saw a window. The bidding went from five to ten and then from fifteen to twenty pound before grinding to a halt. Everyone looked at everyone else for a few moments until a big, red faced farmer called out 'Fifty pound!" A flurry of excitement ran round the hall, but nobody made anymore bids and the farmer grinned expectantly.

"Fifty pound I'm bid from John, Mr. John Trotter over there," called the vicar, "fifty pound, going, going..."

Herbie reached into his shirt pocket, pulled out a crumpled cheque book and waved it commandingly in the air.

"One thousand pound," he boomed.

There was a gasp and then a stunned silence. The champagne bottle wavered in the vicar's hand.

"Did I hear one thousand pound?" he croaked.

"One thousand pound," affirmed Herbie.

"One thousand pound to the tall gentleman with the copper brown hair at the back." The vicar paused. "Going, going, gone to Mr...."

"Watson, Herbie Watson," called Herbie, as he strode towards the stage with the crowd falling away reverentially on either side of him.

At the front of the hall he borrowed a pen and, leaning on a table, wrote out the cheque with a flourish. Then he joined the vicar on stage. He handed him the cheque and collected the champagne, holding it to his chest and bowing slightly to the crowd, as if he had just received a Grammy. A wave of enthusiastic applause rolled through the hall. He held up one hand in a graceful appeal for silence.

"Ladies and gentlemen, it is not you who should thank me, but I who should thank you. This wine is cheap at the price considering what I have seen today. Good people, prepared to uphold their customs and traditions, who contribute to the society in which they live. People who like to give as well as receive. I salute you." He tucked the bottle under his arm and clapped the audience. They responded with another roar of applause.

"As it happens, I am doing a gig tonight in the King's Head at the other end of the village and, if any of you like good music and good beer, we would be pleased to see you there. Whenever I get a break in my busy touring schedule, I pop down and do a little folk club somewhere and donate the money to charity. No matter how careful we are, a few of us fall through society's safety net and I can assure you that tonight's money is going towards keeping someone special off the street. I had better be getting back. Maybe see some of you later." More applause and the vicar leapt forward and shook his hand fervently.

"Wonderful, wonderful, I'll be there and I will try and persuade as many people to join me as possible,"

"Cheers, vicar," said Herbie, then a thought struck him and he turned to the crowd. "Any of you who do come will get another crack at this champagne, I'm going to raffle it during the break."

On his way back to the club he whistled quietly to himself, completely unconcerned at his casual deception of the locals. If it worked, fine, if not, no harm done. The only problem was the cheque, he didn't like the idea of losing twenty five quid when it bounced, but maybe he could work something out.

At the folk club there were about thirty punters sitting in frozen silence as a floor spot quietly went through the motions. He gave Fred a big grin as he joined him standing at the back of the room.

"Great day for the race," he whispered.

"What race?"

"The human race. Didn't you see that film?"

"No, there is one more guest spot, then you're on."

"OK," he said.

A few minutes later, Fred introduced him as "a man well known to you all who really is, er, quite good."

A polite hand as Herbie stalked majestically to the front of the room and picked up his guitar. He threw off a few blues runs to mark his territory and went into the first number. In the background he thought he heard, then he was sure he heard a trooping of feet on the stairs, like the lost tribe of Israel coming home. Out of the corner of his eye he saw the vicar paying at the door with a bunch of people behind him. Bingo! he thought, and drifted into 'Turn your money green' - with feeling.

The first set went down well and at half time the relaxed buzz of conversation showed that the audience felt it was at a happening gig. People can only really enjoy entertainment if there are enough other people there to convince them of their good taste.

Herbie persuaded Fred to raffle the champagne on behalf of the vicar along with the cheap bottle of English wine he and Hettie had donated to help bump up the proceeds for the club. The champagne took fifty quid which Herbie immediately tried to give to the vicar.

"Here you are, mate, stick that in your bin for the tower."

"Mr Watson, this is too generous, I really can't accept..."

For a moment Herbie wavered, then his conscience kicked in.

"No, vicar, take it, fair's fair, you deserve something for bringing all these people down."

One refusal was all the vicar was constitutionally able to make.

"Your generosity is an example to us all," he said.

The petrol gauge was knocking empty when Herbie pulled his battered Volvo off the motor way and drifted into Heston Service Station. He put in twenty pound's worth of fuel and then went over to the all night restaurant for a coffee. The place was nearly deserted and the six or seven customers who were there were half asleep. He took his coffee to a window seat where he could see his car and added up the profits from the evening.

Fifty two people including the vicar, plus thirty normal punters, that made eighty two at a fiver each - four hundred and ten pound. Seventy percent of that was two hundred and eighty seven pounds. He had sold ten CDs that made another hundred, minus the money to the record company, but he had already paid that so it didn't count. A grand total of three hundred and eighty seven pounds. Then, of course, there was the cheque he had given to the vicar. When that bounced the bank would charge him twenty five or thirty pounds, but that still put him three hundred and fifty seven ahead. He took a sip of coffee and sat back in his chair with a feeling of quiet satisfaction. It just shows what can be done, he thought, if you know how to work the angles. A pity to disappoint the vicar, but still.

He needn't have worried, an unexpected six month-ly P.R.S. royalty payment for £1,200 went into his ac-count the day the cheque cleared, so the vicar got his money and Herbie, along with two hundred other peo-ple, got his name on a plaque set neatly into the wall inside the repaired church tower.

CHAPTER 2
THE EX FACTOR

The phone rang, loud and insistent. The form in the large double bed lay stubbornly inert. Herbie Watson was not in the habit of answering early morning calls, unless he was catching a flight somewhere. He opened one eye, saw that it was ten thirty and closed it again. After a few minutes the ringing stopped. He sighed with relief and prepared to sink back into sleep. Then it rang again. The process was repeated until five to eleven when he reached a weary arm out to the side table and picked up the receiver.

"Yeah?" he whispered.

The voice on the other end of the line would have been light and sexy, if it hadn't been quiet and ominous.

"The alimony, Herbie, where is it?"

"Cyn, you know better than to phone me at the crack of dawn, I drove all the way back from Sheffield last night after the gig."

"Good, that means you've got some money. I need eight hundred."

"Eight hundred?" he choked.

"You know as well as I do you haven't paid me anything for two months."

"Yeah, but the car had to be repaired, the gigs are down to a trickle and the record company is going slow on royalties. You don't want to see me on the street, do you? Have a heart." He paused, there was silence at the other end. "No, I suppose that would be asking too much. All right, I'll see what I can do."

He put the phone down and lay back on the pillow, staring at the ceiling. A picture of Cynthia as she was when he first met her came into his mind. She had been a beautiful seventeen year old with light brown, almost blonde hair, an innocently cheeky expression and a pale spray of freckles across the top of her nose and under her forget-me-not blue eyes. She had had the body of a young Aphrodite and a sharp witty intelligence to match. He had met her at the Cambridge Festival, she had hitched all the way from Cornwall and had no where to stay. Herbie always felt responsible for his fans, especially when they looked like Cynthia, so he had arranged a room for her at his hotel. Two weeks later they were married.

He found out later that she had never heard of him before she met him, but by then he was so in love his ego was able to withstand the shock. It wasn't her fault if his record company's publicity department couldn't get their act together.

They had bought a broken down old farmhouse in Kent and renovated everything but the garden. Herbie liked the mysterious dreaminess of overgrown paths and dandelion and daisy filled lawns, cut once or twice a summer. The projected studio in the barn never got built, but there was a work room with half a dozen guitars and an upright piano. They had had two children, Marlon and Flower, and Cynthia had started a herb farm.

For four years everything had been fine, then Herbie began to indulge in the occasional infidelity when he was far from home and under the influence. Cynthia, who had always complained of loneliness during his long absences, suddenly stopped complaining and he had refused to put his mind to the problem of trying to work out why?

The final straw came after a party at the farmhouse when Cynthia told him he had behaved so disgracefully with a friend of hers that she refused even to discuss it. Unfortunately, he had been too drunk to have any clear recollection of what he had done, so the final reason for his divorce had always been a blur.

Overnight, his pretty wife turned into a pretty good accountant - with a lawyer. She got the farmhouse and the children. He got a rented flat in Fulham and the alimony payments.

He climbed out of bed, threw on a pair of jeans and a corduroy shirt and made himself some tea. With the mug in his hand, he went over to a drawer and dug out a packet of dark Virginia rolling tobacco, he told himself he was a man who didn't smoke much, but when he did he liked something he could taste. He saved it for special occasions, moments of stress, or times when he really needed to think, this was all three. He flopped onto the settee, rolled up a thick one, set a match to it and went to work.

The problem was simple, pay-up or face lawyers and bailiffs. It was the solution that wasn't quite so straight forward. He had about two hundred in the bank and the rent was paid till the end of the month, but then he had to live and it was five days before his next gig. How about the horses, he mused? Not exactly a sure fire thing if his recent form was any indication. A bank loan? But that way madness lay. No, there must be something he could sell, or some friend who owed him from way back, after all, eight hundred wasn't the moon. Then he remembered the piano.

Bob Harwood's workshop was a converted railway arch up a cobbled alley off the Wandsworth road. It had a heavy wooden frontage, with a line of dirty windows at the top and big double doors in the middle. On one of the doors, now open, was a printed sign saying 'Harwood Pianos'. Herbie parked the Volvo behind a dented, paint worn Luton van that had once been dark blue and went inside.

Strong smells of polish, turpentine and sanded wood vied for supremacy. Pianos placed, seemingly at random, covered most of the available space. At his yelled 'hello', a tall boney man with dry, dusty skin, dry, dusty, tousled hair and wearing a varnish smeared apron, appeared from a wood framed, glass fronted office. He was grinning through a mouthful of cheese roll.

"Do me a favour. If it ain't 'erbert Watson. Come into the boardroom."

In the old days, Bob Harwood had been a keyboard player on the circuit. He and Herbie had become friends, and remained friends, probably because they had hardly ever worked together. None of Bob's bands had ever crossed over into the money, so in the Eighties he had started the piano business, although he still gigged occasionally on the week-ends.

The office had two chairs, a computer and a phone. A wooden work top, littered with papers, ran along two sides. On the work top, in front of one of the chairs, lay a half eaten cheese roll and a mug of tea. Herbie took the other chair and pulled out his tobacco.

"Snout?"

"Cheers, when I finish me roll. What can I do you for?"

"How would you like a Steinway upright, perfect condition?"

"How much?"

"Eight hundred."

"I'll take it. Why so cheap?"

"Because you have to help me pick it up."

"That's no problem, I've got a trolley and the van's outside."

"It's down at the farm house. Cyn's got it and she'd play hell if I asked her for it, even though it's mine, so we have to be a bit subtle."

"You want to roof your own gaff? Nice one."

Bob pulled the van over on to the grass verge and switched off the engine and the lights. The narrow, hedge lined road leading to the farmhouse was suddenly quiet in the darkness. An owl hooted from a distant tree.

"I hope Cyn leaves like you said," muttered Bob, "I'd feel a proper Charlie if we bumped into her."

"Don't worry, I've arranged to meet her and the kids in the pub in the village in about ten minutes to buy them a meal and give her the money. I reckon we've got about half an hour after they leave the house to grab the piano and get me to the pub before she thinks I've stood her up."

"I'm surprised you haven't suggested we synchronize watches. Got a cigarette?"

"Sure. Hang on. Here she comes."

Headlights flickered against trees. They both ducked down and, a few seconds later, a car drove slowly by and disappeared into the night.

"OK," said Herbie, beating a tattoo on the dashboard, "Let's go!"

The engine kicked into life and they bounced off the verge and back on to the road. Three hundred yards further along, Bob swung the van in through two wooden gate posts with no gate. He floored the accelerator down the drive and slid to a halt in front of the house. They leapt out and, while Herbie unlocked the front door and switched on the lights, Bob got the trolley from the back of the van. He had almost reached the door when he met Herbie coming back out.

"No piano."

"Shit!"

"It must be somewhere. Let's try the barn."

They ran over to the barn, but there was a new steel padlock on the doors.

"Quick," growled Herbie, "back the van up and throw me a rope, we'll have this bastard off in no time."

"Right."

Bob got some nylon tow rope from the van and flung it over to Herbie before leaping into the cab and reversing to within two metres of the doors. He threaded the rope through the lock, tied both ends to the tow bar at the back of the van and stood clear.

"Let her go," he called.

Bob revved the engine in first gear and pulled forward. There was the crunching sound of tearing wood, the lock hit the ground and one of the barn doors shuddered open. Herbie sprang through the gap.

"It's here," he yelled. Come on, lend a hand. You can drop me at the pub on your way back to London."

Cynthia and the two children were sitting at a corner table when Herbie arrived. Cynthia was ill at ease, she hated sitting in pubs on her own. Her smile was one of chilled steel. Marlon looked bored and barely acknowledged him. Only Flower smiled back at his grin and conspiratorial wink as he walked up.

"Wha' cha'," he said.

"You're late." said Cynthia.

"Train was delayed. Did you book a table?"

"Yes, for twenty minutes ago, but I don't think they are very busy."

Not very busy was an understatement, when they went through into the back room they found they were the only people eating. They sat down and he handed Cynthia a bundle of fifties.

"Eight hundred," he said, with quiet pride.

He had hardly got in the door of his flat when the phone rang, it was Cynthia and she sounded as if she had been crying.

"Herbie! We've been burgled."

"No!"

"We got back after dropping you at the station and the first thing Marlon noticed was that the barn door was open. He went over to close it and saw that the lock had been broken and the piano was gone."

"The piano! THE piano! You mean MY valuable Steinway. Anything else missing?"

"No, the house wasn't broken into. I'm so sorry, Herbie, I know how upset you must be."

"Don't worry about it. As long as you and the kids are all right and there is nothing else gone, we had better just take it for luck."

"That's very nice of you. I must admit, I thought you would be more annoyed. But we might be able to get it back, I know who did it."

"You do?"

"Yes, when we were on our way to meet you, there was a van parked at the side of the road not far from our gate. I thought it looked suspicious, so I took the number."

"You did?"

"Yes, and I'll bet it's them. I am just about to phone the police, only I wanted to phone you first to see if you had the serial number of the piano or anything."

"No, of course I haven't. Now listen, there is no point in contacting the police. They will just stand around asking a lot of useless questions and then go home and do nothing. And that van was probably some perfectly innocent bloke having a kip, or checking a map. It's my fault, I should have brought it up here a long time ago."

There was silence for a few moments at the other end and Herbie grimaced. He could almost see the light dawning in Cynthia's mind.

"That dodgy keyboard player, what's his name, that you used to bring down here occasionally, he has a van, hasn't he? He moves pianos."

"Bob? I suppose he does. What's that got to do with it?"

"Don't try and fool me, Herbie," she said. "Why didn't you just tell me you wanted your piano? Am I so difficult to deal with? We had better keep this between ourselves. If anybody found out that you had broken into your own house to steal your own piano, they would think you were a lunatic."

"I was trying to avoid an argument. You know how you get upset over nothing."

"Upset! Have you any idea what it is like to be burgled? I have been living in a state of nervous terror for the last half hour. Upset! There was I thinking you were behaving like a gentleman, coming down and giving me the money, buying us a nice meal, and it was a nice meal, I'm not saying it wasn't, but all the time you were just using it as an excuse to sneak your piano back. Well now you've got it and you're welcome to it."

"I haven't got it," he said, in exasperation, "I sold it. All you have to do is ask for eight hundred and it comes to you out of thin air. With me it's not so simple, I have to do something to get it."

There was a pause.

"Oh, Herbie, I didn't realize. I know how you loved that piano - even though you haven't used it for years."

"It's all right," he said, coming the generous martyr, "you and the kids are more important."

"There is only one problem. Marlon has been learning to play. He has really been coming on recently. If he gets a worthwhile interest, it is up to us to encourage him. Do you think we should get him another one?"

Herbie sighed. "I'll see if Bob's got something cheap and cheerful."

"Thanks, but I don't expect you to bear the expense of this all on your own. I want to contribute something."

"Really?"

"Yes, it's only fair. I will replace the lock."

CHAPTER 3
WAGES

Herbie Watson walked slowly along the lower Richmond Road looking at the numbers. He was wearing dark sunglasses, the collar on his jean jacket was turned up and he hadn't shaved for three days. Every ray of hope had been extinguished and he had been forced to surrender to the continuous ebb tide of circumstance. In his darkest moments he had never thought it would come to this. His scariest nightmares had not included the scenario. He had to get a job.

It was his friend, Bob Harwood, the piano restorer, who had finally hit the bottom line and suggested it. After listening to a long diatribe on finance, or the lack of it, from Herbie he had said: "Why not try working for a few weeks, until the gigs start rolling in again. Come on, it's not that bad, it won't kill you."

He came to an entrance between two houses that led down to a small yard. Tacked up on one side of the entrance was a printed hard board sign saying: Painting Unlimited Ltd. He turned into the yard and was confronted by a neat pile of ladders and two vans. Behind these were some white painted workshops and storage spaces. A narrow iron staircase led up to a reception and offices on the first floor of what was obviously the main building.

He explained at reception that he was the man who had answered the ad and was shown into a partitioned office with thin, vomit green industrial carpet, plastic chairs, a table and a desk. Behind the desk a big man, wearing a big grin was standing holding out a meaty hand.

"Mr. Watson? I'm Dingo Summersbee, g'day."

Herbie knew immediately that he was in for a heavy dose of Antipodean charm and prepared to defend himself. He went into the handshake like a wrestler going into a clinch.

"I think I spoke to you earlier, Mr. Summersbee."

"Too right. Call me Dingo, Herbie. Now, let's see if we can sort something out."

He handed him a form to fill in which asked about personal details and experience. This didn't take long as Herbie had been a full time musician for the last twenty years and nothing he had done seemed to fit into any of the boxes. He had once had a job painting offices in the dim and distant past and he tried to make this fact look as central to his life as possible. It was all he had to offer in the way of qualifications.

He gave the completed form back and Dingo checked it through.

"So you're a muso," he said, looking up, "I used to be a drummer myself, great fun, but then I had to make some money."

"Really?" said Herbie. Knowing he was in the presence of another failure didn't make him feel any better, and such a happy failure at that.

"We pay a fixed fee on every job," continued Dingo, "so the quicker you do it the more you make. We've got a school to do over in Mitcham. Here is the address. I'll meet you over there tomorrow morning at eight." He stood up and held out his hand. "Glad to have you aboard."

At a quarter past seven the next morning an old Volvo could have been seen nosing its way over Battersea bridge and into the sprawling mass of South London. The car was taking a while to warm up and it kept cutting out. Herbie hugged the cold steering wheel and resigned himself to restarting at every traffic light. He understood, he didn't like early rising either.

The school was deserted when he drove in through the rusty iron gates and parked near the front entrance. He got out of the car, lit a cigarette and looked around.

Even in the brightness of the early morning sunshine the surrounding link fencing gave the feel of a low security prison. Not a very successful one, he thought, with a smile, there's been a massive break-out. It was the late October half-term.

At eight thirty Dingo rolled up in a brand new small van that like him looked as if it was for show rather than work.

"Sorry I'm late, I've been rushing around like a blue arsed fly. I've got the keys here somewhere. Right, let's go."

He opened the door and they went in to the cold desolation of an empty school, only fractionally less depressing than the manic loneliness of a full school. Dingo led the way to a large sports changing room containing showers, lockers and rows of hooks. A musty smell of sweaty football shirts, and socks hung in the air. Herbie looked bleakly around and Dingo rattled his keys.

"I reckon there's four days work in this," he said, "I can give you three fifty. You should be able to get a screw out of that."

Rapid calculations on Herbie's part got him nowhere, it had been too long since he had done any painting and decorating. But even if it took him five or six days, he thought, it still wouldn't be too bad.

"Sounds fair," he said, giving the narrow eyed stare of the hard negotiator.

"You're on. The paint and dust sheets are in the back of the van. There's another guy doing the main hall, should be in by now, he's got the ladders."

Five minutes later Herbie started work. That is he sat down on a paint can surrounded by new smelling brushes, rollers and dust sheets and had a cigarette. On closer inspection he could see the job was a nightmare, special gloss paint for the showers, a ceiling criss-crossed with wooden slats which precluded using a roller, radiators, pipes and windows everywhere. Well, there was nothing else for it, he threw away his cigarette and pitched in.

After four days, he had done the showers - badly - (plenty of smears of gloss paint on the concrete floor which would be a devil to clean up) and the ceiling, two mind numbing coats with a brush over an acre of slat-ted plasterboard.

He was working nine or ten hours a day flat out and he could see it was going to take him the rest of his life to finish the job. As he started wearily on the walls, he came to the grim conclusion that he had been stitched up. A joke was a joke, but if he carried on at this rate his daily wage would be down to a pittance. The whole thing was too much like work, as he remembered it. Getting the sharp end of the stick when you're young is one thing, but at his age it wasn't so funny.

All he wanted was out, but if he packed it in now he would get nothing. Summersbee would put in another mug to finish the job and Herbie could go fly a kite. Well, the bastard wasn't going to get away with it. Herbie mulled it over while prodding his paintbrush moodily at a radiator. Half an hour passed and his mind was still a blank, clogged up with dust, paint fumes and the prospect of endless toil. Suddenly, he came to a decision. He was going to go home, have a shower to get the paint out of his hair and then have a few dust clearing pints down at the local. Maybe things would look better in the morning.

The Cat and Fiddle was round the corner from his flat and just across the Fulham Road. The outside had been painted brown in the dim and distant past and the faded gold letters of the name were almost indecipherable. Inside it was dark, somnambulant and comforting. Herbie bought a pint, sat down and gave himself up to reverie. He toyed with the idea of never going back to the job again. No more white spirit, no more paint in his hair, no more cleaning of clogged up brushes, he would be a professional musician again. True, there was the little matter of rent and Cyn might come after him for some alimony, but maybe he could work something out. But all that could be decided tomorrow, a time that seemed to be in the almost unimaginably distant future. Right now, all was peace and life was a dream.

"Anybody sitting here, mate?" A tall cavernous looking man with long dark hair streaked with grey was standing by the chair on the other side of the table. A shorter, fatter, younger man was behind him. Herbie shook his head and gestured that the seats were free. He was on his third pint and he had not noticed the pub filling up around him. The two men sat down with their drinks and immediately became involved in a discussion about the days racing.

"I reckon McCoy pulled Nightmare. She had dropped a class and the rest of the field was rubbish. She could have won that race on three legs with a blind jockey facing the other way. Instead of which she comes in fourth and no pay out."

"You're right there Phil."

"Course I'm right, but it don't matter, a nod's as good as a wink. The next time out she's a certainty and the odds will be well up. We'll be pissed for a week."

"You're right there Phil."

"Course I'm right. Now, are you getting them in or what?"

The younger man got up to get two more pints while Phil looked around with haunted, restless, dark eyes.

"Why didn't you use a brush?"

Herbie glanced up and saw that the remark had been addressed to him.

"What?"

"You got paint in your hair."

Although this pleasantry was presumably supposed to be humorous, there was no hint of it in

Phil's expression, which remained impassive and interrogatory.

"Been doing a bit of painting and decorating," said Herbie.

"The curse of DIY," said Phil, with disgust, "people think they can do it and they can't. Meanwhile, us professionals are out of work."

"You're not going to get much competition from me," said Herbie, "after this job, I'm jacking it in."

"Yeah? What are you doing?"

"A school, showers and changing area. And it's taking me bloody forever."

"Yeah, now me and Tosh would knock something like that out in no time, wouldn't we Tosh?" he said to the younger man as he returned with the pints.

"You're right there, Phil."

Herbie's paint spattered hair quivered as he leaned forward, an idea dawning in his mind.

"I reckon there is still two day's work there for two people," he said. "How much would you charge to do it?"

"Cash? Hundred each. You supply everything, including the next round of beer."

If these two bozos could finish the job for a couple of hundred, Herbie reasoned, he would be out of it and a hundred and fifty to the good. Not a great result after all the work he'd done, but a result. True, Phil struck him as a bit of a psycho and Tosh was no polymath, yet a man had to use the materials at hand and painting and decorating wasn't quantum physics.

"O.K." he said, "you're on. I'll meet you outside the pub at eight tomorrow morning to take you down there." And with the cool expansiveness of the entrepreneur, he fished into his jeans for the money for three more pints.

The next morning he took them down to the school and showed them the job.

"Can you do this in two days?" he asked.

"Piece of piss." said Phil.

"Right," said Herbie, "I'll be down tomorrow afternoon with the money."

"How about a sub?" said Phil. "Me and Tosh are stony after last night."

Herbie dug deep and came up with two twenties. "There's forty," he said, and humming quietly to himself, he drove home and went back to bed.

The following day he pulled up at the school at three o'clock in the afternoon. He got out of the car and strolled towards the door, rattling his keys. He felt clean and comfortable in shining boots, faded jeans and an old leather jacket, clothes that had never seen a day's salaried work in their lives. He wandered along the corridors to the changing room whistling softly to himself and thanking his stars he was out of it. He had spent the day on the phone trying to set up a few gigs in between intervals of playing the guitar and listening to Robert Johnson. He had made a pact with himself, if he was going to go down, he'd go down singing, not waving a paint brush. He jerked open the swing door to the changing room with a cheery, "How's it going fellers?"

The words died on his lips. The scene that confronted him was devastation. The whole room could have been picked up and moved to the Tate Modern as an art exhibit without changing a thing. Paint tins lay all over the floor knocked over or upside down. Dust sheets swirled and eddied in kicked up confusion. The pasting table was a mass of paint lids, paint encrusted brushes and gloss covered rollers. Paint seemed to have got everywhere except on the walls and window frames where it was supposed to have gone. The room was as silent as a graveyard.

Herbie moved forward, stepping carefully to avoid getting paint on his boots. Over by one wall he saw a lump of dust sheet with a paint spattered shoe sticking out. He stepped closer and looked down. It was Phil, curled up and sleeping like a baby. Nearby, spread-eagled on his back, so covered with paint it looked like camouflage, lay Tosh, as relaxed and oblivious as a dead man.

Herbie shook Phil by the shoulder and got no more than a groan, a shrug and a settling to a deeper sleep.

He tried again, harder this time and longer. Gradually, Phil came reluctantly and irritably to the surface.

"Whass er matter? For Christ's sake. Can't you see I'm tired?"

"Close," said Herbie, "but you got one letter wrong. Fired is what you are. Can you hear me? FIRED!"

"Whass 'at? Fire. Where? What? Phil stumbled to his feet, peering about and sniffing warily, but Herbie had turned away and was kicking Tosh on the sole of an upturned shoe, slowly and methodically. In a few moments, Tosh too had come round and was sitting up scratching his head with a dazed expression on his face.

Herbie picked up an empty bottle of vodka that was lying on the floor at his feet and stared at the chaos around him, noticing for the first time what looked like hundreds of cans of Special Brew among the debris.

"All right you two, out. It's back to D.I.Y. You professionals have done enough."

"What about our money?" said Phil.

"You've had forty quid for doing nothing but damage. I think we can call it quits."

Phil walked slowly over to a line of hooks on the wall and took his jacket off one of them. Slowly, trying not to move his head, he put it on.

"Come on Tosh. I'm not saying nothing, but If he 'finks I'm going to let some poncy bastard steal the bread out of the mouths of working men, he's got another 'fink coming. Am I right or am I wrong?"

"You're right there Phil," said Tosh, and with that the two shuffled out the door.

Herbie sighed, spread out one dust sheet and began throwing the rubbish on to it. All he could do was clear up as much as possible and start work again tomorrow. He was back to square one only now he was forty pounds and two pints down on the deal. It did not make him happy, but he was philosophical, it was his own fault for hiring a couple of unstable drunks.

"Christ! What's this, Herbie, kiddies play week? What you been doing?"

Dingo Summersbee was standing just inside the door regarding the mess with the disgruntled expression of a prop forward who has just watched the other side score a breakaway try.

"You're right, Dingo old son, it's a total piss off. I had to pop up to see my agent at lunch time and some kids must have broken in and trashed the place."

"If this was kids, I'm Kylie Minogue. Look at all those tubes. I didn't realize you were Heavy Metal. It's a miracle this room is on the ground floor and there are no TVs to throw out the window."

"Good gag, Dingo, but no cigar. I had nothing to do with this, but I know it's down to me. I'll sort it out."

"No, I'll sort it out. I'll get a couple of guys in tomorrow. You're off the job."

Herbie threw one more can into the heap.

"O.K. What do I get for doing all I've done so far?"

"The milk from my granny's tits - zilch."

For a few moments Herbie considered dumping a can of paint over Dingo's head, then he rejected the idea as childish. In a way, he was relieved. Losing the money was bad, but the prospect of getting out into the cool air and away from all this almost made it worth while. Without bothering to say another word he walked to the door and out into the fading light of a now chilly, October evening.

There was an expresso coffee maker hissing on the cooker, Bach on the record player and a showered and changed Herbie Watson taking down a bottle of Martel from a cupboard in the kitchen. Everything was coming back into focus. Harvey Small, who ran a blues club in the West End had booked him to fill a cancellation in a couple of week's time and Cyn had agreed to hold off on the alimony until after the gig. Somebody had phoned up about guitar lessons and, best of all, his latest song writing royalty statement had been lying on the mat when he got home, five hundred smackeroonies sitting in his bank account. He poured out a black coffee and laced it generously with brandy. He took a sip, just right, this was going to be a mellow evening.

A long ring on the door bell split the silence and jarred his mood of quiet introspection. He put down his coffee and strolled to the door.

"Hello, mate, I just came round to apologize. Me and Tosh were well out of order." It was Phil, gaunt, unshaven and looking about as apologetic as a hungry hawk.

"Forget it," said Herbie, "water under the bridge."

"You're a diamond. Look, let me in will you? I gotta sort this out for you, I'd never forgive myself if we parted in bad blood."

Herbie stood aside. "I've having a coffee in the kitchen - want some?"

He led the way to the kitchen, poured Phil out a coffee and pointed to a stool. Phil sat down.

"I said to Tosh you were a good bloke, strike me dead if I didn't. I sez to him I sez, Herbert won't see us starve. We'll finish the job tomorrow and we won't charge him an extra penny for it. Now, you can't say fairer than that. I'll go round there now, I said, and tell him we don't welch on a deal. I'll sub a few quid for food and fares and tomorrow we'll turn that place out clean as a whistle."

"I appreciate that Phil. It does you credit, but I'm off the job myself. We'll just have to take it for luck."

"You can't back out now, Herbert, we've offered to make good. We had a deal."

"There's nothing I can do about it, Phil, you and Tosh got me fired.

Phil thought this over for a moment, narrow eyed and scheming, then he came up with a solution.

"O.K. Give me the rest of my money and I'll go."

"I don't want to have to say this again, so I'm going to say it slowly. There is no job, no deal, no money - nothing. Finish your coffee and leave."

Phil leapt off the stool, crashing into Herbie and knocking him against the work top. A knife appeared in his hand and he held it up to Herbie's throat. Herbie noticed that Phil's usually haunted eyes had gone strangely blank.

"You give me my money, you bastard, or I'll slit your fuckin' throat."

This, thought Herbie, is all I need. He wondered if Phil was bluffing, or if he really was crazy enough to do it. He decided not to find out.

"All right, mate, take it easy. You'll get your money, just put the knife away before someone gets hurt." He thought it might be uncool to specify who that someone was likely to be.

For a moment, nobody moved, frozen in a grotesque tableau, then the light of understanding gradually re-appeared in Phil's eyes and he stepped back.

"All I want is my money," he said, in a low, almost apologetic voice.

"Right, I understand, but I haven't got it on me and I won't be able to get anything until tomorrow. Look," he picked up the royalty statement and hand-ed it to him, "there's five hundred here that should clear in my account tomorrow afternoon. I'll meet you down the pub in the evening and bring the cash with me. I want this thing sorted out and no come backs."

"How do I know you'll be there?"

"You know my address. I'm often in the pub. I'm not going to emigrate to Australia because of a hundred and sixty quid. Do me a favour."

Phil wavered, it looked all right, he obviously had Herbie scared shitless, but there was still the problem of tonight.

"What about a few quid on account," he said, "to show good faith."

"Sorry, mate, I'm flat until that cheque clears."

"Give us a bottle then, Tosh's mother's died last week and I got to bring him out of himself somehow."

"I never keep drink in the house, I'm practically tee-total, but do you know the barman round there?"

"The shaven headed geezer with the earring and the tattoo?"

"That's the one. His name's Murgatroyd, he knows me well. Tell him I said to sub you twenty quid, I'll sort it out with him tomorrow."

Immediately Herbie said this it became apparent to Phil that he was wasting drinking time. He felt he had Herbie right where he wanted him and there was no more to be said.

"I'll be creepin' then. Don't bother to see me out, I know my way."

"It's no bother," said Herbie, following him to the door, "I'll see you tomorrow about seven o'clock."

He shut the door, bolted it and went straight back to the kitchen. He had suddenly started to feel sick. He opened the cupboard, took down the brandy and poured himself a large one while trying to remember the barman at the Cat and Fiddle. He hardly ever used the pub and doubted if he had spoken to him more than twice in his life. I wonder, he thought, how he will take to being called Murgatroyd and being asked for twenty quid.

The following evening he walked into the pub with two plain clothes policemen. Phil was sitting in a corner studying the racing page. He looked up and saw Herbie.

"Hey!" he said, "that bloke's name ain't Murgatroyd."

"That's him," said Herbie.

There were no preliminaries, they didn't even say hello. The two policemen just jumped on Phil and pinned him to the floor with his hand behind his back. Then they searched him and took his knife away. They had him handcuffed and away in a police car in little more than thirty seconds.

Later, it turned out he had only recently come out of jail after doing ten years for stabbing someone to death outside a pub in the old Kent Road.

"We can get him on the knife," the sergeant told Herbie, "and with his record and the fact that he is still on parole, he will probably go down for it. There were no witnesses to his assault on you, so I doubt we can make that stick. Count yourself lucky to be alive."

He had not long got back to the flat when Bob Harwood phoned.

"How's the job going?" he asked.

"I got fired."

"Oh well, you can't win 'em all. Listen, it may have worked out for the best. There's a bloke I know wants the outside of his house painted, four or five day's work and good money, it's a natch."

"No thanks."

"Why not for God's sake? It won't kill you."

"I wouldn't be so sure about that," said Herbie.

CHAPTER 4

HOW NOT TO TOUR ITALY

I t was a bitterly cold winter's day and Herbie Watson had his boots up on the fender in front of the gas fire soaking up the heat, while he sat comfortably back in an armchair reading a Sherlock Holmes story. It was two days after Christmas and he had nowhere to go and nothing to do. He was persona non grata down at the farmhouse in Sussex where his ex-wife, Cynthia, and his two children were spending the festive season, and, as a sporadically working folk musician, his friends were scattered far and few.

He was taking a sip of Navy Rum from the glass at his elbow when the door knocker sounded three bone shaking raps. There being no Mrs Hudson to help him, he got slowly to his feet, went out into the hallway and opened the door.

A beautiful girl was standing there hugging a sheepskin coat to herself against the cold. She had auburn hair surrounding a finely boned face, a pale olive complexion and large brown eyes.

"Mr Watson?"

He nodded.

"I have to talk to you. It is very important.."

This bore such a striking resemblance to the story he had been reading that he waved her in before he knew what he was doing. He resumed his seat in the armchair and watched her take off her coat and sink into the seat opposite him. She was dressed in teenage battle gear, big boots, black jeans, black polo neck and an imitation silver tooth necklace.

"I am Antonia Genovese, you know my father, Giovanni Genovese."

The light dawned. Gino, as Herbie knew him, was a big wheel in the Italian acoustic scene and the owner of a club in Rome where Herbie occasionally played. He was a paunchy, black jowled man, heavy with continental gravitas, who had a tendency to drop dark hints about his dubious political connections. It was hard to imagine him as the father of the girl sitting in front of him, but, even if he was, did that give her the right to invade his home and start bending his ear? With some difficulty he concealed his irritation beneath an air of polite interest. After all, a gig was a gig.

"Good old Gino, how is he?"

"OK. When I left he gave me your address as someone to contact as a last resort. Obviously, he knows you are a busy man."

Herbie doubted if that was the reason, but he managed the long suffering, patient smile of a man in a hurry detained while he waited for her to continue.

"I came to London a few months ago to do a course in art and design at St Martin's. I didn't like it and after a while I stopped going. I didn't tell my father because he would have told me to come home. For a month everything was fine, but then my father must have phoned the college, or something because he found out I was no longer attending the lectures. Of course, he ordered me to come home and when I refused he sent me a plane ticket and stopped sending me my allowance. I cashed in the ticket to pay my rent and tried to get work as a model, but none of the agencies were interested."

Herbie sighed, he saw it coming, she was going to put the bite on him, for sure. Even so, he didn't like the idea of this girl wandering around London destitute.

"So you're broke," he said, "All right, I'll give you the money to..." He paused. "No I won't, I'll buy you another ticket, take you to the airport and put you on a plane to Rome. Me and Gino go way back."

He noticed her visibly relax, beauty and charm had worked once more. She moved slightly in the chair, conscious of her femininity and smiled.

"Can I have a coffee?" she asked, suddenly, getting to her feet.

"Of course." He started to climb out of his chair.

"Don't move, I'll make it myself. Do you want one?"

"Cheers. The kitchen is just down the hallway."

He watched her walk through the door like a young colt and reached for his tobacco. She has got to be eighteen or twenty, he mused, as he rolled up. Then the stolid, stoically cynical face of Gino loomed in his imagination and he put the thought out of his mind. More problems and less gigs were things he did not need.

Antonia returned with the coffees and gave him his, but she didn't sit down. She paced the room, holding her cup in both hands for warmth. Herbie watched her while he smoked. Finally, he worked out why she was so restless.

"I'll take you to the airport as soon as you have finished your coffee," he said.

"I don't want to go to the airport," she replied, "I had another reason for coming to see you."

She sat down again and peered into her coffee cup.

"I met a photographer who seemed very nice. He told me he had contacts at all the top modelling agencies and he promised to get me work. When the work came through it turned out to be nude modelling.

45

He said it was just bread and butter stuff while he was waiting for some real assignments and I believed him. Anyway, I was desperate.

"At first it wasn't too bad because we were friends, at least I thought we were, and he made it easy for me. But after a few sessions, he wanted me to work with other girls and with men. I didn't feel comfortable with the idea, so I quit."

"You made the right decision. Come on, let's get down to the airport."

"Wait a minute, I haven't finished. He wants me to pay to get the photos back."

"What, for a few silly snaps? Tell him to stick his tripod up his Nikon."

"You don't understand, I did those pictures thinking it wouldn't matter. Even if he managed to sell them to some stupid magazine, it was very unlikely that anyone who knew my father would see them. I was wrong, he found out that my father had money and was involved in politics. If these photos were published in Rome, it could damage my father politically. As you know, he is very strongly on the left and his opponents could easily use me to make him look bad. Especially as he is in the middle of some important elections at the moment. Denny, the photographer, knows this and is trying to use it to get me to get money out of my father, or someone, but I can't."

"How much does he want?"

"£5,000."

"You're right, you can't."

"That is why I came to you, you are my only hope."

Herbie's thoughts flickered back to Sherlock Holmes. He too was the last court of appeal. He too had beautiful women asking for his aid. The parallels were too obvious to be ignored. Besides, he wanted to help old Gino because, with any luck, that would help old Herbie. A tour of Italy next year would do no harm to the schedule.

Denny McKenny, the photographer, lived in a square of sleepy suburban houses near Turnham Green. He was tall with long, brown, curly hair and a red face that looked as if it had got that way from drinking. He wore a check shirt and blue jeans and had the nervous, hurried enthusiasm of the hustler.

"You're the guy that phoned, right? Come in. I haven't got much time, I have got a session at two."

As he said this he was leading Herbie down the front hall to a room at the back that had been turned into a studio. It had bare floorboards painted black, blacked out windows, backdrops, reflectors, heavy lights and not much else.

"I use this as a blank canvas," explained Denny, "from here I can go in any direction I like. What sort of style are you after?"

"Oh, kind of film noir with an early French Cinema Verité atmosphere," said Herbie, through his sunglasses.

"No Problem. Who put you on to me? Did you see that photograph of mine in last month's Stud?"

"No, I've heard your name around. You seem to be building quite a reputation."

"Yeah, you've got to be able to do the business in this business. Too many fuck-wits around with a lot of front and no talent."

"That's good to hear. I need someone who can work quickly and come up with a useable product. The guys at the record company are putting pressure on me, they want the album out before the American tour in March."

Pound signs started floating in Denny's eyes. This could be his big break. No more cheap shoots with girls who thought that all you needed to do to become an actress was take your clothes off. He became suitably serious and low key.

"I might be able to move a couple of sessions and fit you in sometime in the next two or three days, if it's urgent?"

"You're a real buddy. You're totally saving my neck here, Denny, and I won't forget it. Let's say two o'clock on Wednesday. One more thing, I tend to get wound up at photo shoots, its some kind of neurosis. I might bring a little coke to help us relax. Is that a problem?"

"It doesn't bother me. In fact, I occasionally use it myself. It puts the girls in the mood, when a session just isn't happening."

Herbie cracked a craggy smile and held out his hand.

"That's what I call service. And by the way, I don't want any haggling over money. If the shots are good, I pay top dollar and that is that. I'll see you Wednesday."

They shook hands and Herbie ambled out to the street, climbed into the old Volvo and pointed it towards home.

When he got back, Antonia had cooked dinner and looked as comfortably at home as only a girl can look in someone else's flat. She had showered and was wearing one of his shirts loosely over her jeans. She greeted him casually as she moved about cutting up salad and stirring a saucepan, giving her impression of the complete kitchen Madonna. Herbie was pleased, despite his reservations about her 'Germany invades Poland' approach to his territory. It had been a long time since he had smelt the warm, gentle odours of a well prepared meal and heard the sound of company on opening his front door.

The meal was Spaghetti Bolognese and salad with a bottle of Chianti. Antonia had a good appetite, it was obvious she hadn't been eating well lately.

"I've arranged a session with Denny for Wednesday, I'll give a friend of mine, John, a ring to come round and give me a hand. He runs a private investigation agency, but he used to be my ex- band's manager, so he won't mind doing me a favour - even if I have to pay him."

"OK."

Her reply, as she worked on the spaghetti, showed complete acceptance of his handling of the situation, to the point of disinterest. Herbie was annoyed. Ever since he had agreed to help, she seemed to have dismissed the problem from her mind. Here she was, living in his flat, sleeping on his sofa, handing him her troubles to sort out and it was all as if it were nothing. Of course, her confidence in him was gratifying, but a little bit of awe and admiration would have been nice.

"You ought to get wise to yourself, young lady. You're playing with fire, going through life with this laissez faire attitude of yours. One day you'll fall and there will be no one to catch you."

She looked up, her mouth full of spaghetti, an expression of frozen, pained surprise on her face as she regarded him with solemn eyes. Was this reality, censure, disapproval coming her way? She didn't know what he was talking about, but she sensed a note of criticism and she didn't like it, it made her feel vulnerable and exposed.

Herbie had seen the same look on his daughter's face when he tried to correct her and it always defeated him. It defeated him now. He gave a strained laugh and picked up the Chianti bottle.

"Well, we can worry about that some other time. More wine?"

She nodded, then, trying to please him said, "I tidied up the flat while you were out. There was a pile of old newspapers in the corner, some of them must have been years out of date. You're like my father, a real old magpie."

Herbie choked on his wine. It wasn't just the fact that she had called him old, those newspapers contained articles about him that he had been meaning to cut out for his publicity folder. He leapt up and sprinted for the front door with the vague suspicion that this was the day the rubbish was collected growing stronger by the second. He was right, there wasn't a rubbish bag in sight. He walked back inside.

"Lost to history," he said.

"Anything valuable?"

"Measured against the background of an unfolding universe, no, otherwise, yes. Have you seen my tobacco?"

"Tobacco? There wasn't anything left in that packet, was there?"

Herbie picked up the phone and tapped out a number.

"Denny? Herbert Watson. We've got a problem. I haven't been able to get in touch with my connection, he's on holiday in Colombia, or somewhere. We might have to cancel the session. It's a total piss off, but I don't think I can handle it straight. The snaps won't be any good if I'm not relaxed." He paused for a moment, listening. When he spoke again his voice was full of gratitude. "You can? You're a star. A couple of hits is all I need... OK, I'm back on board, decks cleared for action and all set for take off. See you tomorrow."

He put the phone down and looked at the man sitting opposite him.

"We've got a live one," he said.

The day was sharp and cold and there were light flurries of snow in the air. Herbie rang the bell with a frozen finger and hunched into his jacket, glancing round at the bare wintery trees in the square. Denny opened the door full of fake bonhomie.

"Hey! my man, now we're cooking with gas. Coffee's on."

He turned and led the way into the kitchen which was along the corridor and past the studio on the left. Herbie closed the door carefully, putting the Yale lock on the latch as he did so. Then he followed him down.

They sat on either side of the kitchen table with their coffees and Denny took a plastic bank bag containing white powder out of his pocket. He laid a small, framed bathroom mirror flat on the table and shook a little of the cocaine onto it. Then he divided it into two lines with a razor blade.

"I had some of this last night," he said, "it will blow your head off."

Herbie winced, that meant it was probably cut with amphetamines. Denny took his wallet from his back pocket and flicked out a crisp, new, ten pound note. He rolled it carefully into a cylinder and handed it to Herbie.

"Be my guest," he said.

Herbie pushed one nostril closed and, using the ten pound note, sniffed up a line of the coke with the other. He felt a tingle at the top of his nose, then a rush to the head. Definitely cut with amphetamines, he thought, as he handed the note back to Denny and watched him follow suit. They were sitting there, enjoying the blast, nodding slowly at each other with dazed grins on their faces, when a voice spoke from the doorway.

"You're under arrest, McKenny. You are not obliged to say anything, but anything you do say will be taken down and may be used in evidence against you."

Herbie had never seen anyone straighten up so fast. Denny's smile changed into a look of frozen horror and he spun towards the door. A well dressed man in a dark coat over an expensive grey suit was standing there with his hands in his pockets regarding them with a quizzical eye. He was about forty, good looking, and wore his prematurely greying hair swept back in a debonair wave. There was an alive tension about him that belied his sober dress and made you feel that here was a man who enjoyed conflict and excitement. He moved into the room, baring his teeth in an aggressive grin.

"That got your attention. Luckily for you, we're not talking law - yet. My name is John Hawkes. I am a private investigator working on your attempt to blackmail Antonia Genovese and, looking at this cosy little scene, I don't think I'll have any trouble sorting it out."

Denny was still trying to put the pieces together.

"How did you get in?" he expostulated.

"Nobody heard my knock, the door wasn't closed properly, so I pushed it open. Now, we can do this the nice way or the hard way, to me it makes no difference, to you it's the difference between freedom and two or three years in jail."

But all the fight had not gone out of Denny. With a mounting sense of outrage, he pushed back his chair and started to get to his feet.

"Get out!" he roared.

Hawkes' open palm hit him on the shoulder and knocked him back into a sitting position.

"Have it your own way. We'll just take this little lot down to the police station and see what they have to say about it. Why don't you give me a bit of fun and tell me I couldn't do it?"

But something told Denny he could do it. That was always the way, millions lifted by graft every year, he tries a small business proposition and the sky falls in. He was pissed off with the whole thing.

"OK. If I delete the photos, that will be the end of it, right?"

"Certainly."

He led the way into the studio, got the images up on his computer and ceremoniously deleted them.

"There you are," he said, "now everyone's happy."

"Yes," said John, drily. "Of course, you know her father is an Italian politician. The family originally came from Sicily, I believe. He can do favours and he can get favours done, if you see what I mean, so if you have got these photos backed up, it might be a mistake to let them see the light of day."

"I haven't, I swear I haven't, on my life."

"Exactly," said John.

As Antonia was leaving to board the Air Italia flight for Rome she gave Herbie a big hug.

"Thank you. I will tell my father how much you helped me. I hope to see you in Rome the next time you play there."

"Sure. I'll give him a call after the elections, maybe we can fix up a few dates."

She turned to John.

"And now I have my own private detective to call the next time I'm in trouble."

"Make it soon," said John, with a grin.

She smiled and ran towards the boarding gate.

Ciao.

Once she was out of sight Herbie and John strolled towards the bar.

"Were you serious when you mentioned payment?" asked John.

"Of course," said Herbie.

"How do you want to do it, cash, or through the books?"

"Anyway you like. Things are a little tight at the moment, so we might have to wait for the Italian tour, but it's as good as in the bank."

John laughed. "You forget, I used to be in this business. You wait for the Italian tour, I'll take a double malt now."

"John, I wouldn't think of it. That's very decent of you, mate, are you sure? I tell you what, I'll throw in a copy of my new album 'Killing the Blues', how's that?"

"Thanks. You'd better make that whisky a triple."

A week later the phone rang, Herbie picked it up and Gino's heavy, guttural voice came down the line.

"I have to thank you, my frien', for being so kind to my daughter. We would love to see you in Roma."

"I'd love to see you too, Gino."

"I may be able to arrange some dates in April, or May."

"Sounds great. By-the-way, how did the elections go? I hope the right side won?"

There was an ominous pause, then the slow, heavy voice again.

"Yes, the right did win. This is a bad line, I will call later."

The line went dead and Herbie put the phone down. There was nothing he could do. There was no point in phoning back to try and explain the nicities of English to an irate Italian Communist. He just had to take it for luck. Maybe sending him a red scarf for Mayday would help.

CHAPTER 5

BIG JOHN'S COMING TO TOWN

"Hi Herbie, it's Brad. Hey man! Saturday night. Why ain'cha working?"

"I had the Albert Hall only I cancelled it. Some sixth sense told me you were going to call."

"What? Oh yeah, right. How's it been going anyway?"

"I'm totally wasted. I've been so busy it's unreal." Herbie tucked the phone between his shoulder and his ear and began to roll a cigarette. He could keep this up all night.

"That makes me feel good. Hey! I left the Wabash Agency and started on my own. I'm now Brad Brainstorm Productions."

"I like it and, while we are on the subject, why don't you produce a few gigs for me? I haven't played State side for quite some time."

"Hey! that would be great. Herbie Watson pipes the main stem after all these years, oooee, that would be something. Just like Woody and Cisco. I gotta tell you I admire you, Herbie, you old pros ain't never gonna lie down."

"I wasn't thinking of hoboing, Brad, I was thinking of paid work."

"Paid work! Mmm, there's a thought. Let me run with that. But the reason I called is I'm doing the bookings for Big John Tucker now and he has just signed a distribution deal with Helluva Records in England, they're crazy about his music."

"I've never heard of him. A Johnny come lately is he?"

"Hell no! He used to hang out in the Village in the old days. He's got all kinds of credibility."

"Even so, what's it to me?"

"Hey! That's the Herbie Watson I know. I call up for a little advice and right off the bat you're offering to help. I need to work him in on something quick, just a little showcase for the guys at the record company and to kind of get him off the ground in London. If you had a West End gig coming up, he'd love to open for you."

Herbie sat slowly up in his chair. It was a long time since an American agent had phoned him and here was one asking him for a favour. Could this be made to run two ways?

"As it happens, Brad, I have got a gig in two weeks time at the Crossroads club, but that's too soon."

"No, it's perfect, right when he's gonna be in town. Can you ease him in?"

"I don't know. It won't be easy at this late stage. Of course I want to help because I know how much you believe in friends working together."

"You said it, bud. Helping a friend is the biggest pleasure in friendship, I reckon."

"I couldn't have put it better myself." Herbie paused, allowing time for the unspoken words to wash back and forth across the Atlantic. It didn't take long, Brad was quick on the uptake.

"I could maybe see about some festival work for you in return."

"OK he's in. I'll phone Harvey Small, he's the guy who puts the gigs on at the Crossroads."

"Herbie, you're a star. Catch you later." Brad rang off.

A week went by in which Herbie went about his business. He played a couple of out of town gigs, backed a few slow horses and had a call from Lorine, an old girl friend, who was coming over from California for a short tour with a quartet.

"Maybe we can meet up, if our gigs don't clash," she had said.

"You bet," Herbie had replied, who remembered her as tall, blonde and friendly.

It turned out she was free on the night of the Crossroads gig and that made it perfect. It would prove to her that he was still in the West End and still a head-liner after all these years. True, the club was a little on the small side, although that was not how he would have described it, he would have preferred words like 'exclusive', or 'cult', or perhaps 'for the aficionado', no doubt he would use them all during the course of the evening when he met up with Lorine.

Usually, Herbie did not take much interest in the run up to gigs. His agent sent through the posters and publicity and sometimes arranged an intcrvicw at a local radio station and that was that. He would turn up on the night and it either went well or it didn't. This time it was different, he had two reasons for wanting it to go well. Good feed back might make Brad more enthusiastic about booking the American gigs and he wanted Lorine to see him in the best possible light. There is nothing more forlorn than inviting someone along to a gig where the audience looks as if it has been decimated by the Black Plague the night before. He phoned Harvey Small ostensibly to check if the posters had come through, but really to find out how the tickets were selling.

Harvey's voice was light, dreamy and abstracted, he always sounded as if he was about to say something definite after many wanderings, wonderings and umms and aahs, but he never did.

"Oh, hi, yeah," he drawled, once he had established who he was talking to, "the posters are up. We're getting some interest, a few people have called to find out what time Big John is on. It's understandable, he played with pretty near everyone in the old days. You've probably got him in your record collection somewhere.

Maybe, thought Herbie, but I had a record deal of my own.

"That's great," he said, "so we're getting some action. I thought it would go all right."

"Yeah, I was thinking of putting Big John on at ten thirty."

"But the main spot starts at ten and my set is longer than half an hour."

"You could go on at nine thirty."

Something rotten in the state of Denmark, thought Herbie, this didn't make sense. It would have been too late to advertise Big John, which meant that, apart from word of mouth by the guys at the record company, anyone who came would be coming to see Herbie. There didn't seem to be much point in putting an unlisted guest on in place of the main act. He would have to give it some thought. Meanwhile, he wouldn't come the prima donna.

'I don't mind going on at half nine," he said, "but I'd have trouble finishing before a quarter to eleven. If that suits you, it's OK with me."

"That will have to do then," said Harvey and hung up.

Herbie ground his teeth, reached for the Navy Rum and poured himself a stiff one.

The night of the gig Herbie got to the club at six o' clock to do the sound check. His poster was there in the window beside Big John Tucker's. On the sign board outside were the words 'Tonight, Big John Tucker' and underneath 'Plus Herbie Watson'. Inside he saw Harvey rushing around in an excited manner. He bounced over and shook Herbie's hand.

"Great to see you, Herbie. I've got to go. We'll have a beer later."

"What's the idea of the sign outside, I thought this was supposed to be my gig?"

"Oh, I know," said Harvey, grimacing as if the whole thing was totally beyond his control, "but the people from his record company can't get here till late, Brad's been phoning me all week about it. But it doesn't make any difference, it's still your gig as far as I'm concerned." And with that he was gone.

Typical agent, thought Herbie, as soon as they get a contact they're off yelping like fox hounds and Harvey was a sucker for the old bullshit. Well, wait till the performance, he would show them who was the player round here. He went past the bar and into the room where they held the show. It was dark and dismal, the only light seemed to be coming from over the mixing desk in the corner. A tall man wearing jeans, T shirt and a dead pan expression came towards him.

"Tony," he said, his lips barely moving, "I'm doing the sound."

"That makes me feel better, Tony, we worked together before, remember? My name's Herbie."

"Yeah, I think so. What do you need?"

"A microphone and I'll D.I. the guitar."

Herbie took out his old Gibson and climbed on stage. In a couple of minutes they had the sound about right and he had just unplugged when he heard a yell from the doorway.

"Hey! How you doin'? Tony, right?" A tall, lanky man advanced into the room with his hand held out. He wore a fur lined flying jacket and had his guitar slung over his back in a soft case, which brought a sneer to Herbie's lips. Tony came out from behind the desk and such was his enthusiasm he almost woke up.

"Big John?" he ventured as he shook the other's hand.

"Sure. Neat little club you got here."

Herbie climbed off stage with his Gibson, walked over and stuck out a hand.

"Herbie Watson," he said, with magnificent understatement.

Big John went into the hip handshake of slapping palms and grabbing thumbs and what not that Herbie had never quite got the hang of.

"Yo, bro. Caught your sound as I came through the bar. I thought, might even have a little trouble going on after this guy. I love that old stuff."

"Yeah," said Herbie,

He went back to the dressing room, which wasn't a dressing room but a sort of lumber room full of paint stained wooden trestles, bits of chip board and old paint cans left over from some totally unnoticeable decoration carried out by the club. He cleared a space, perched on a trestle and began to roll a cigarette. A sudden involuntary shiver ran through him and he looked around for some form of heating. There wasn't any. The place was as cold and bleak as a pharaoh's tomb. He cupped his hands to catch the momentary warmth from his lighter as he lit his cigarette. You can see where musicians are on the social scale in this place, he thought. He was contemplating gathering a few bits of rubbish together in the centre of the room and starting a fire, when the door opened and Big John came in having done his sound check. He unslung his guitar and stashed it beside Herbie's.

"Hey! This place is so funky, it's unreal. Know anywhere round here I can get something to eat, preferably with some kind of heating apparatus which it ain't against their religion to turn on?"

"Good idea," said Herbie, temporarily burying the hatchet in the interests of survival, "I'll show you."

He led the way to a Cypriot restaurant on the corner of Charing Cross Road. There were few customers this early in the evening, so they could sit where they wanted. Herbie selected a table up a few stairs at the back as sufficiently incognito. Before sitting down he called back to the counter.

"Hey! Nicky, how are you, mate? A bottle of house red when you're ready."

"Paulo, I'm Paulo. I'll be with you in a minute."

Big John took off the sunglasses he had put on as they were leaving the club and flung his flying jacket casually on to the inside seat. Then he sat down with studied unconcern. Nobody noticed.

Hey! I could eat a hog."

"Not in this place," said Herbie, "Lamb or Chicken."

"Jewish, huh?"

"No, Greek. I think it's because Greece was once part of the Ottoman Empire."

"Do tell." Big John stared gloomily at the menu in the hope that a plate of ham and eggs had slipped through the net in the name of freedom.

Paulo came with the bottle of house red and two glasses. He poured out a glass for Herbie, but before he could go any further Big John held up a meaty hand.

"I guess I'll have a mineral water," he said, in the underplayed, but underlined, mission statement way of the reformed alcoholic.

Herbie immediately offered his tobacco, convinced he was on sure ground. He was, Big John didn't smoke either. They ordered two shish kebabs and Big John leaned back resting his arm along the neighbouring chair, as if he was putting a confidential arm around the world.

"Yeah, I climbed out of the bottle about five years back. It changed everything around. My life now is incredible, I've got everything going for me."

Herbie took a big gulp of wine and lit a cigarette.

"Yeah, Herman Bourbon has just covered a little song of mine called 'Tippin' Turpentine Triple Trouble Blues', he's putting it out on his new album. The thing that got me was, you know, that song ain't easy to sing. I thought he might be better off doing 'Fresh 'em up Frank and let the Fur Fly'."

Herbie raised an eyebrow and poured himself another glass of wine.

"But no, man, he aced it. Course I got new management now. This guy could sell sun lamps in the Sahara. In fact, that is a bone of contention between us. 'You know, Big John, ' he says to me, 'I'm losing my edge, your act's just too easy to sell.' Heh, heh. He's on the committee at Newport, so I should get the festival next year."

The food arrived and Big John relapsed into what could hardly be called silence as he started to eat. Herbie didn't mind, at least it interrupted the catalogue of good fortune. The next thing was who had to have the most chilli sauce on their food. They ladled it on while swapping tales of chewing raw chilli in sleepy bars watched by startled Mexicans. Eventually, the chilli bowl was empty and, rather than order another, they tacitly agreed to a red faced draw.

"The problem I got now." said Big John, when he finally pushed his plate away, "is I'm so busy I don't hardly get back to the ranch. But I'm happy to do it 'cos that means I can afford to play little clubs like this one every once in a while. Life ain't all take out, you got to put back too, or the scene dies."

"Yeah." said Herbie.

"Hell, I know you agree, I can't believe a guy like you needs to play places like this for money. I mean you're a legend. Do you know your records are damn near unobtainable in the States - rare as hen's teeth? They're collectors items, man."

But Herbie wasn't going to take that lying down.

"You know, I'd heard that," he said.

"Huh?"

"There's a record store in the Village in New York that will pay fifty dollars a copy for my album 'Killing the Blues'."

"Well, I'll be... Fifty dollars!"

"Crazy, isn't it, when I'm selling them for ten quid a piece over here?" Smiling philosophically, he turned and ordered a large brandy.

When they got back to the Crossroads, the bar outside the music area was heaving. Herbie's initial glow of smug self satisfaction was slightly dimmed by the chorus of yells saluting Big John, who was brought to a halt by back slapping recognition and offers of drinks. Herbie moved on. God! How I hate sycophancy, he thought.

He found Lorine at the other end of the bar in a shadowy corner underneath a stair well. Although at the moment in poised repose, holding a glass of white wine in two shapely hands, she radiated Californian sun tanned vitality.

"Hello, Lorine."

"Hey! Herbie. Great to see you. What a cool crowd, it seems you haven't lost your touch."

"Well, it's a small club. They have probably had to turn people away."

"Wow!"

Herbie eyed her closely. That was one of the few things wrong with Lorine, she could be very sarcastic. The trouble was her baby blue eyes made her look so innocent it was difficult to tell.

"Yes," he continued, "I like to do these little places now and again, it gives me a chance to put something back."

"That's the Herbie I remember," she said, reverently.

When he started to play, half the crowd went into the music area to watch, while the other half stayed resolutely in the bar drinking and talking loudly. When he had finished Big John came on and they swapped over. Back in the dressing room Herbie was putting his guitar into its case when Harvey Small came in and shuffled through the rubbish towards him. He was wearing a soft, smirky smile.

"Knock out set," he said in hushed, awed tones. Then after gazing at Herbie in starry eyed wonder for a few seconds, he snapped out of it and started to talk business.

"You drew fifty people. Tickets ten quid. We take fifty percent. You get two hundred and fifty. Quiet night. Maybe you'll sell some CDs."

Herbie straightened up. "This place must be smaller than I thought. It looked like a hundred to me."

Harvey shifted furtively. "There was a hundred, but fifty of them were with Helluva Records and came in on the guest list."

"What? You mean those bastards didn't fork out for one ticket?"

"It's kind of a record launch from their point of view and they are interested in promoting more stuff down here."

"Well it's kind of a gig from my point of view and that pissed bunch of make weights probably stopped some of my crowd from getting in. It may have slipped your mind, but I am supposed to be a professional musician. I play for money."

"Right, Herbie, and here it is, two hundred and fifty." Harvey pressed a wad of notes into his hand. "You did the booking. It's your gig. Whatever you sort out with Big John is fine with me." And he wafted out the door like smoke following a draft.

Herbie was counting the money morosely when Lorine came in.

"Hey, man, wow, that was beautiful. It was wonderful to hear you play again."

As a one time girl friend she understood the balm he needed to soothe his eternally wounded soul, but for the moment he was beyond even flattery.

"You won't believe it," he said, "they let Big John's entire audience in for nothing."

"Jeepers! You can't allow that, go out there and throw them out."

Nice idea, but scarcely practical, he thought.

"No, somebody might get hurt and it wouldn't be fair to break up Big John's set. But the bastard's not getting one broken down penny of my money for this, I'll see him starve first."

Even as he was talking he began to hear his words as they must have sounded to Lorine - mean minded, money grubbing and what was worse - poverty stricken. They did not sound like words from the Herbie Watson front office, words to bewilder a beautiful woman. And, of course, there was Brad, was it wise to leave him out of the equation, he still might come through with some work? He changed tack.

"Still, I arranged the gig for him as a favour, I'm not the man to back out till the job's done, no matter how he behaves. Anyway, what's two hundred and fifty quid? Rat shit. It's not worth arguing over."

"Wow, Herbie, you've changed. If somebody treated you like that In the old days you'd have hated him for years."

"You're right, I've learned the hard way, some people never learn. You've got to look out for the other fellow when you get the chance, I always say." He tilted his jaw, stared flinty eyed into the distance and gave her the old 'working stiffs unite' look. She delicately pushed a paint can aside with her foot and came towards him.

"I'm so glad I came," she said, "if I hadn't seen it with my own eyes, I never would have believed it."

They were still there, sitting side by side on a paint trestle when Big John came back stage after finishing his set.

"Hey! I could eat a hog. Say, them little old boys out there sure love the blues, don't they?"

"I expect that's why they signed you," said Herbie. He stood up and handed over half the money. We made two hundred and fifty between us, the blues lovers didn't cough up a red cent."

"Well I'll be... Why didn't you say so, I'd a told them to haul their asses out of there, record company, or no record company?

The door opened and a burly figure with close cropped hair wearing a dark suit, dark shirt, no tie and a long black coat leaned into the room.

"Big John, we're off now. Lovely set, mate. Give you a buzz in the morning."

Big John spun round. "Sure Joe. Nice seein' ya. Thanks for coming down." He turned back to Herbie and Lorine as the door was closing. "Hell of a nice guy," he said loudly, and then much quieter, "he owns the label."

"We'd better get going," said Herbie. He picked up his guitar case and pointed out a black hold all to Lorine. Would you mind taking the CDs?"

"No, not at all."

"Now, hold on there." Big John was leaning back on his heels, big and expansive. "That was some playing you did back there, Herb, just beautiful."

"Cheers."

"I got friends back in the States I know'd be tickled to death to hear you, so why don't I take a few CDs back show them what it's all about?"

"How many do you want?"

"Ten."

"Done."

A hundred pound went into Herbie's pocket and ten copies of 'killing the Blues' passed into the hands of Big John.

"Catch... I mean, see you later," said Herbie.

When they got outside, Lorine noticed he was smiling quietly to himself.

"What have you pulled to look so smug," she said, "and what made him buy all those old CDs?"

"No idea," he replied, "I expect he did it out of pure good heartedness. Now, how about some iced champagne and a slice of toast?"

"Good God! Where would you get a combination like that?

"My place," he said.

"That's the Herbie I remember," she laughed, "only who gave you the champagne?"

Three days later Brad phoned.

"Hi ya, Herbie, nice going, man, Big John said you did him proud. We'll do some more, lots more. Listen, about the work we were discussing. I got you a festival. It wasn't easy and the money's still up in the air, but they want you big time. It's the Navajo Arts and Crafts Spring Festival, something to do with the Corn God. Beautiful location, right on the reservation, only a hundred miles into the desert from Albuquerque. I told them you were related to Grey Owl. You do Red Wing, don't you?"

"No."

"Rain dance?"

"No."

"Well, do one of those crazy morris dances, they'll never know the difference. It'll be great."

CHAPTER 6
MY PAL ROCKY

Herbie Watson swung his old Volvo off the road and on to a dusty track and followed a line of cardboard signs to the artist's car park. A T-shirted student type checked his name against a list, gave him a pass sticker for his car and waved him through. Pulling up on the shadowy side of a transit van already baking in the late morning sunshine, he climbed out and breathed in the atmosphere. A fee of one thousand pounds. He could smell it on the breeze. Across the fence was an array of tents and stalls and in the distance he could hear sounds of fiddle music echoing from the main stage. The Little Mimsey Festival was already under way. Putting on his sunglasses he strolled round to the entrance.

"Herbie Watson," he informed the man on the gate.

"Got a ticket, chief?"

"I'm playing this evening."

The man lost what little interest he had had in the acquaintance.

"Ask for Henrietta at the Information Tent, she'll sort you out." He waved a vague hand in the direction of nowhere in particular and turned to another customer.

The festival was not large, maybe a couple of acres. One main tent and one side tent took care of the music the rest was hot dog vans, arts and craft stands and a beer tent. The crowd at this point in time was perfunctory.

Henrietta turned out to be a sharp faced, bespectacled woman of about forty five, busy as a bee and drunk on power. She bustled up to the Information Tent soon after he had enquired for her carrying a clip board and wearing a thin cloak of superficial friendliness.

"Ah, Mr. Watson," she said, "I've got you down for a guitar workshop tonight and then main stage tomorrow at three o'clock and six o'clock on Sunday."

Herbie gave her a blank stare, two dead beat spots when everybody would be drinking beer in the sun and distributing messy fast food wrappers around the grounds while waiting for the real music to start. This wasn't quite how his agent had described it. 'Main stage both nights, mate, beautiful spots, better than the headline when everyone will be too pissed to care, free accommodation, hospitality tent, it's like money from home.' He raised his sunglasses and unleashed the personality.

"That sounds a little early, doesn't it?" he said, "I've got a very valuable guitar, I like to keep it out of heavy sunlight."

"Oh, I know, but we've had to shift things around a bit. We've got a new headline act, he's a big American star, evidently. He's played with people like Ry Cooder and Dave Bromburg, one of his songs is up for a Grammy. They say we were lucky to get him - Big John Tucker."

That make weight again, he seemed to be everywhere these days. Herbie dropped his sunglasses back into place.

"That's a pity," he said, "I was jamming with Rocky a couple of days ago and he thought it might be fun if we did something together on the Sunday, but six would be too early for him to get here. He's in the studio all afternoon."

Henrietta's nose quivered like a magnetic needle finding true north.

"Rocky? Do you mean Rocky Hill?"

"Sure, he's a friend."

"But that would be wonderful. What a perfect way to close the festival."

"Listen, it's just a jam, we don't want to cause any fuss. You don't have to worry, I am one of the few people who have heard of Big John and I can tell you he's great. I'll phone Rocky tonight and cancel."

"No, don't do that. Leave it with me and I'll see what I can do. Here is the address of your accommodation, it's about a half a mile along the road into the village. Your workshop is at five thirty in the little tent." And she reeled away muttering, "Rocky Hill here, I can hardly believe it."

Herbie allowed himself a grim smile and wandered back to his car to drive down to the B & B. His lie had been an instinctive reaction to what he thought was a stitch up. If you didn't fight your corner at these penny ante festivals you got treated like dirt. Actually, it wasn't all fantasy, he did know Rocky Hill slightly. He had supported him on a few gigs in the old days, in fact Herbie had once borrowed a tenner from him to buy petrol to get home. And then there was the time Rocky had given his 'Killing the Blues' album a mention in an interview. It wasn't exactly friendship, but it was close enough to make Herbie not feel guilty about misusing his name.

He checked into the B & B and was shown up to a small tidy room with a sink a dressing table and a double bed. The landlady told him the breakfast times gave him his key and retreated. The house relapsed into the silence of a Welsh Sunday. He looked at his watch, he had a spare hour before he had to go down to the workshop, so he took off his boots, sank on to the bed and fell asleep.

The workshop consisted of showing people who couldn't play the guitar and didn't really want to learn, a few finger picking patterns and illustrating them with songs. Herbie's method was to do the minimum of explanation with the maximum of demonstration, he felt that singing songs was easier than painstakingly going round the class correcting faults. After he finished he was as dry as a chord encyclopedia, so he made his way over to the hospitality tent for a beer.

"'ere! What's this about you and Rocky Hill?" His friend Bob Harwood, the keyboard player, was standing at the bar regarding him quizzically.

"Keep your voice down," said Herbie, "it's supposed to be a surprise."

"Surprise! I'll say, I didn't even know you knew the geezer."

"Oh, we go way back. Listen, keep it to yourself will you? I only mentioned it in passing, I don't want Rocky to think I'm making capitol out of his name."

"Perish the thought, but you don't have to worry about me, I've got a session in London tomorrow. I'll be playing here again with a band on Sunday night, though, I'm glad to say, I wouldn't want to miss this."

"Great," said Herbie, "I'm looking forward to it myself."

By the next day word of the scheduled impromptu jam had done the rounds of the festival and Herbie's stock had risen accordingly. People he didn't know he knew were greeting him with familiar nods and friendly grins. He only had to walk into the hospitality tent to have a pint of beer poured out and waiting for him by the time he got to the bar. Henrietta was continually liaising with him, making sure that everything was all right and assuring him that she was doing her best with the billing. By the evening it was all sorted out and she was able to tell him that he plus special guest (giggle) were headlining the following night. Herbie acquiesced gracefully. "If that is the way you want it?" he said and then proceeded to regale her with one or two anecdotes featuring him and Rocky, usually to the detriment of Rocky and the aggrandizement of Herbie. In fact it was all going so well and everybody was getting so much fun out of it that Herbie considered adding Spence, Rocky's bass player, to the ensemble, but regretfully decided against it. If he built expectations too high, the come down would be harder and more difficult to explain. All was joy unconfined until late that evening when Bob Harwood returned from London.

Herbie was sitting in the bar after his set, which had gone down so well that he had almost found it irritating. He felt himself being engulfed by the shadowy form of the superstar. The real Herbie Watson seemed to be fading to be replaced by a new more aggressive illusion. Now that he was known to hobnob with the great they saw him as if lit by some ethereal afterglow.

A man who had access to a luminous world where they could not follow. Everything he said was funny, everything he played was brilliant, until Herbie had begun to lose his grip on his performance. How could he fine tune the music if there was no sounding board? By making everything he did equally valuable it somehow had became valueless.

He took a sip of beer. Oh well, only one more day to go. At this rate it didn't seem to matter whether Rocky Hill turned up or not, his name and peoples own imaginations were enough. Still, he did not want to let them down, he would make up some story that would set their ears on fire and by the time they came out from under the ether he would be gone. He thought for a moment then he had it. Rocky Hill had phoned him not half an hour before to say he had been held up. Mick Jagger had called to say that Robert de Niro was in town and wanted to discuss the possibility of the Stones and Hill collaborating on his new movie project. If he finished the meeting in time he would still try and make it blah, blah, blah. Herbie was just sinking a beer congratulating himself on this one when Bob Harwood swam into his ken like a grubby, unshaven planet.

"Ah, the legendary Herbie Watson. May I join you?"

"Leave it out."

Bob placed his beer on the table pulled up a chair and sat down.

"How did the session go?"

"Good. You'll never guess who was in the next studio to the one I was in."

"No, who?" Herbie couldn't have been less interested.

"Rocky Hill."

"What!" Herbie's beer slurped on to his jeans and he held the dripping pint away from his body.

"Yes, naturally I told him how I was looking forward to his appearance down here."

But Herbie was once more inscrutable. "You shouldn't have done that, you know how sensitive these guys are. What did he say?"

"Well, he didn't seem to know much about it. He just looked at me for a moment and then he said, 'Typical, bloody Watson.' Then he walked off muttering something about lawyers."

"Jesus Christ! That, if I may say so, is typical, bloody Hill. You just can't trust him. Everything these guys say is like it was written on water, even they couldn't tell you what it was two seconds later." He paused and then started laughing quietly to himself. "Good old Rocky, you've got to hand it to him, he nearly got me going that time."

Bob Harwood eyed him suspiciously. "All right, what now? If it's so funny, let me in on it."

"You don't get it do you?"

"No."

"He was ringing your bell, he's such a wind-up merchant. That clinches it, he'll be here for sure."

"Yeah, I'll bet." Bob stood up. "Abyssinia," he said and strolled out of the hospitality tent.

Herbie Watson opened his eyes and immediately shut them again painfully against the glare. He lay there for a moment trying to work out how the evening before had ended and how he had managed to get back to the right B&B, but nothing surfaced. He turned over groaning slightly and squinted tentatively at the crack in the curtains. Suddenly, his head jerked up from the pillow, wide eyed and staring. There was a lump in the bed beside him. He followed the moulded contour up to the pillow and saw a mass of luxuriant brown hair glinting in a sunbeam. Desperately now, he tried to pierce the cloud that had rolled across the night before. 'Who the hell is she?' he thought, 'think Watson, think.' Gradually, vague scenes began to dimly emerge from his memory.

He had had about four pints, then he had moved on to the rum. There had been a lot of people around and he had been stupid enough to hold forth on life as a superstar. He had talked about his band, his hit record, massive American tours, limousines. Famous names had dropped from his lips like jewels from the mouth of the kind sister in the fairy tale. Amidst all the swirl and the flowing drinks there was a beautiful girl paying him too much attention, whispering confidentially in his ear, sitting coyly in his lap and asking him wide eyed questions about Rocky Hill. He hadn't failed her. It almost made him blush to think of the lies he must have told. But after that, nothing, the rest was a blank. Well, there was no use putting it off, he had to find out what had happened. He prodded the sleeping form.

"Morning," he said, far from cheerfully.

The figure moaned, made a stretching motion and sat up. Ruffled hair cascaded over bare shoulders and down to two perfectly formed breasts.

"What time is it?" she said.

"Ten thirty," said Herbie, slightly mollified, at least she was as beautiful as he remembered. "Listen er..."

"Charlotte."

"Listen Charlotte, that beer last night, there must have been something wrong with it, my memory's a bit hazy. What exactly..."

"Nothing."

"Nothing?" He looked down and noticed that he was still wearing his shirt and jeans. "I behaved like a gentleman?"

"If to behave like a gentleman means to be helped upstairs before collapsing on to a bed and snoring loudly, then you behaved like a perfect gentleman."

He moved closer and put his arm around her shoulders.

"I'm sorry, I am afraid I wasn't very hospitable last night."

"You promised to introduce me to Rocky Hill."

His arm fell away. Now Hill was pulling his women for him. Wasn't the smouldering Watson charm good enough anymore? This whole thing was getting ridiculous. Suddenly, he peered closely into her face, a cold fear had begun to clutch at his heart.

"How old are you?"

"Eighteen, why?"

"You're never eighteen."

"Well, I am sixteen, or I will be in two months."

Herbie sprang from the bed as if he had been stung by a cattle prodder.

"What the hell are you trying to do, get me thrown in jail?

"You promised to introduce me to Rocky Hill."

"I wouldn't introduce you to my sixty year old accountant. Do you realize you are young enough to be my daughter. My God! if Hill keeps hanging around like this, I'll have to go teetotal."

"You promised..."

"Stop talking like a faulty cd and get dressed, I have to think. If this gets out it will kill my schools tour stone dead." He walked over to the window, drew the curtain and looked down.

"Hey! I've got an idea. It is only about fourteen feet to the ground. If I hold you out the window by the arms and then drop you, it would only be a fall of a few feet. Do you think you could do that without breaking your leg?"

"I'm hungry, if I don't eat soon, I'll be ill."

He turned around. She was now wearing, trainers, pink lycra pants down to the knee and a loose T-shirt. She was also chewing gum. He brightened up, anything less sexy was hard to imagine.

"All right, we'll go down to breakfast, but remember, you are an old school friend of my daughter's who got stranded. And call me Uncle Herbie. If you do a good job, I still might introduce you to Rocky Hill - if he turns up."

The daylight was fading to the rosy glow of a summer's evening by the time Herbie deigned to make his appearance in the hospitality tent. He had spent the day wandering around the village, resting and making sure everything was ready for a quick getaway after the show. The atmosphere was electric. People he had not seen over the last two days were strolling to and fro, people in hats, Moroccan scarfs and outlandish jackets, with hard drinking faces and blondes on their arms. Where they came from nobody knew, where they went none could tell, but if there was a music business happening anywhere from John O' Groats to Lands End there they were. Herbie acknowledged a few laid back greetings as he moved to the bar carrying his guitar case. He stopped long enough to pick up a pint and then strolled out to the backstage area.

Bob Harwood was sitting at a table with a large whisky in front of him and a big grin on his face.

"Cutting it fine, isn't he?" he said cheerily, "you're on in twenty minutes."

Herbie sat on a chair beside him, took out his old Gibson and started tuning up.

Bob watched him quietly for a moment and then tried again.

"So where is he?"

"How do I know, we're mates not Siamese twins. Actually, we spoke on the phone about half an hour ago."

"What did he say?"

"You'll find out. Be patient."

"Big John Tucker who had finished his set to rapturous applause arrived backstage. He was magnanimous in defeat.

"I tried to warm 'em up for ya, Herbie, maybe I warmed 'em up too much, but you'll soon quiet 'em down. I just love that old stuff you do."

As Herbie stood up with his guitar ready to go on, Henrietta darted in clutching her clip board, looking like a hen that had lost a chick.

"Mr Watson!" The love fest was over. "Where is Rocky Hill?"

"Everything is under control, Hetty, this was supposed to be a surprise, remember." He didn't know if she liked being called Hetty, but he hoped not. The M.C. appeared at his side wearing sunglasses and a Hawaiian shirt.

"O.K. man, ready to go. Let's do it."

Herbie followed him up the stairs to the stage and stood waiting at the side behind the curtain while he was being announced.

"And now, ladies and gentlemen, to close the show, the man you have all been waiting for - (wild applause) Herbie Watson. Raucous cheers and shouts of "Come on, Rocky."

Herbie strolled casually up to the microphone, handed his lead to the sound man to put into the d.i. box, threw off a blues run and went into Sonny Boy Williamson's 'Don't Start Me Talking'. When he finished there was enthusiastic, but expectant clapping. He gave them his 'Davy Crocket grinning a bear' smile and waited for silence.

"There has been a rumour going around this festival about a certain friend of mine that only came to my attention an hour ago. Things have been said that should not have been said. People have spoken who had no authority to do so. But was that your fault? No. Why then, I thought, should you, my audience, suffer. I am in this business because of you, without you I would not be here. I decided to do what I could, even at this late stage, not to disappoint you." There were a few slow hand claps accompanied by restive jeers. "I made a phone call not half an hour ago, ladies and gentlemen, and I spoke..." A huge roar of applause rolled up from the audience accompanied by excited whistles and yells. Herbie rocked on his heels. What was going on? He felt a moment's disorientation and turned to look at the wings. Rocky Hill was walking towards him buttoning on the strap of his acoustic guitar. Another microphone was pulled forward, Hill handed his lead to the sound man and turned to look at Herbie.

"Thanks a lot, mate," muttered Herbie, "listen, none of this is down to me, I'll explain later."

"Forget it," grinned Hill, "I knew this was the only way I was ever going to get my tenner back. Let's play some blues."

CHAPTER 7
DO IT AGAIN

Joshua Marx was a tall, thin, pale faced man with a wispy beard who ran a small independent record company along the lines of a prison farm in the American South. Ostensibly there for the good of society, its real purpose was to make money while keeping a mixed collection of ne'er-do-wells safely occupied. It is not easy, as he would have told you, to make money where other people would starve. It takes talent, your own, certainly, but mostly other people's. His recipe for success could be summed up in one phrase 'cast iron costing'. To him that meant squeezing everybody dry while keeping as much for himself as possible.

His company, Travesty Records, was situated in a drab residential street near King's Cross where a medium sized family home had been converted into his centre of operations. The studio was in the sound-proofed basement. The ground floor had been knocked out and lined with shelves to be used for storage, while his office was on the first floor. This was where Josh hatched his master plans and where he had been known to return a phone call, that however, had been in the distant past and had probably been from his mother.

Today he was looking at the returns for the most recent Herbie Watson album 'Killing the Blues' and they weren't great. Nine thousand five hundred units moved so far and sales had dwindled to a trickle. He was unimpressed, but not surprised. He never embarked on a project without having forecast how many the resultant recording would sell and he was usually right, almost to a CD. In Herbie's case he expected to sell ten thousand and, when the dust settled, he would have done. No, that wasn't why he was dissatisfied. What bothered him was the thought that if the album had been by Herbie's old band Colney Hatch, it would have sold forty thousand. He didn't like the band, he didn't like their music, but in the music business that was hardly a consideration. Forty thousand was forty thousand, that was a consideration. He decided in the interests of his bank account to grace the world with another Colney Hatch CD.

The next question was how to get these tired has beens into the studio, as far as he knew they had not spoken to each other in years. He stood up, went to the door of his office and yelled down the stairs into the vacuity of the warehouse.

"Hey! Space."

A square built man with long hair, a beard and a woollen cap pulled down to his ears appeared from behind some shelves and blinked up at him. Josh hired a few of society's throw backs to push boxes around and Space was one of them. His name probably had more to do with his former drug taking proclivities than the gap between his ears, but Josh thought the name fitted either way.

"Get me a cup of tea and a salt beef sandwich will you, mate?"

Space took an old envelope from his hip pocket, a pencil from behind his ear and wrote laboriously, speaking the words out loud.

"One tea, no sugar and..."

"A salt beef sandwich."

"One salt beef sandwich. Anything else?"

"No."

"Pickle, mustard?"

"I always have pickle and mustard."

"With pickle and mustard. That it?"

"Yes."

"Right, back in two ticks." He didn't move.

"What's wrong?"

"No dosh."

Josh dug out a tenner and floated it down to him. Space caught it with a movement like a goldfish snapping a crumb.

"Cheers. Oh, I done those shelves last night, the ones you asked me to clear. Had to stay late to do it. No time for breakfast this morning. Hope I don't come over all weak on my way to the deli."

"Get one for your self."

"Cheers."

"What are friends for?" said Josh, making a mental note to deduct the price from his wages.

He returned to his desk. That was the trouble with hiring hippie gnomes to work for you, he thought, they practically want an award for turning up, let alone doing anything. Award! His mind locked on to the word like a sprung steel trap. That was it. He would arrange for Colney Hatch to get some lousy award for services to music, then he could come waltzing in like their fairy godmother and offer to put out a reunion album. He reached for the phone.

Herbie Watson was dancing round the flat, punching the air and yelling to no one.

"Yeah! Right on! About bloody time!

Lefty Richardson of 'The Independent Record Company', a trade magazine, had just called to tell him that his old band Colney Hatch had won a special life time achievement award for services to music. Herbie had never heard of the magazine, or the award, but it didn't matter. It was recognition whichever way you looked at it. Over the past few years he had got the impression that everyone had won an award except him.

True worth had gone unrewarded while glib network-ers had garnered all the accolades. Old jealousies had formed new conspiracies to keep him out in the cold. Now, he realized that he had been wrong, everything was for the best in the best of all possible worlds. Justice had been done. Then he saw the off key note in the melody. The band might be expected to play at the award ceremony and, failing a satellite hook up, that meant only one thing. He would have to meet the other members of the band again and, horror of horrors, they might even have to rehearse. At that moment the phone went again. He picked it up and growled out an award winner's "Watson".

"Hello, man, Surrey. What's all this about an award?" Surrey Clayburn was the other guitar player in the band. He had spent the years since the break up making gentle New Agey albums with titles like 'The Faeries under the Mountain' and 'Heartbeat of the Universe'. Except when under the influence of alcohol, he had a laid back persona that concealed a considerable sense of self importance. Your only clue as to what he was really thinking was his humorously condescending sarcasm about anybody who wasn't present and occasionally about those who were.

"It's true," said Herbie, "a magazine called 'The Independent Record Company' has given it to us for services to music."

"So I heard. I don't know if I can associate myself with something like that, I mean too many people know

I'm above this sort of thing. It's not as if the other guys in the band could even play - except you, of course - you know, I mean, spare me."

"You mean you won't come to the ceremony?" There was no regret in Herbie's voice and that was a mistake.

"I don't know. What do you think? I don't want to let the lads down - they would never let me down. Luckily, I'm an amnesiac."

"That's all water under the bridge," said Herbie. "I would have thought that the publicity might be useful for your next album 'Goblin Twilight" or whatever."

"Yeah, right, same old Herbie, but what bugs me is why an award after all this time? I mean who's in it for what, or what's in it for whom?"

"It's just our turn that's all," said Herbie, "everyone else on the planet has got one, why not us?"

"I'll tell you why. We are deader than a filleted mackerel which, let's face it, is fishy. See you at the wake."

As Herbie put down the phone his face assumed a thoughtful expression.

The ceremony took place at the Dead End club off Charing Cross Road. A gaggle of heavy duty security types in black T shirts hung around the door, chatting to each other and looking down on the customers, literally and figuratively. The place was full of independent record company executives and their acolytes and a string of young bands who had also

won awards. The general public had not been invit-
ed, they could read about it later if they cared to - few
of them would.

Herbie got there with nearly the complete band,
Surrey Clayborn, Screech Jackson, the fiddle player,
and Bob Harwood, depping for the bass player, Mitch
Mitchel-Fotheringay, who had last been heard of some
years before when he had been touring with a Heavy
Metal band in the States.

"Right," said Herbie, when they had been shown to
their table at the back of the room, "a quick 'Bonnie
Bonnet' the way we did it at the sound check, then I'm
off. You lot can do what you like."

"And no group photos," said Surrey.

"They're bound to catch you together when you accept the award. What's the difference, anyway?" said Bob.

"It's not so much the lack of prestige, it's the lack
of money," moaned Surrey. "This is Colney Hatch as I
remember it. You're the hired help and you're getting
paid and the band, as usual, are doing the paying." He
turned to Herbie. "What's the matter, couldn't you get
in touch with Mitch?"

"Not exactly," replied Herbie, evasively. "We were
lucky to get Bob at such short notice and you can't expect him to do it for nothing."

"Streuth! I can hear the violins," said Screech.

"If they're in tune, you're not playing them," coun-
tered Surrey.

Bob watched them as they argued: Surrey, large bodied, bearded, like a modern Falstaf; Herbie, still slim, craggy faced, downward lines emphasizing his sardonic mouth; Screech, long, thin, unkempt, slumped forward like a puppet abandoned by his master. All three of them drinking pints of Guiness and rolling cigarettes as fast as they smoked them. Even in their estrangement, there was a unity about them - like fractious brothers.

"On my life! Colney Hatch!"

Joshua Marx was standing in front of them, arms out spread, oily smile, dripping with insincerity.

"It's just great to see you together again. I've always loved you guys. You really deserve this award. There is no question in my mind that you guys made a huge contribution to the history of music. Listen, we've got to talk. Catch you later." And he grooved off back into the crowd.

"What does he want?" queried Screech, as he patted his jacket to see if his wallet was still there.

"I don't know what he wants," said Surrey, "but what he doesn't want is to pay us the royalties he owes us."

At that moment there was a crackle of microphone, a brief searing whistle of feedback and a plaintive "Is this one on?" to warn people that the business of the evening was about to commence. Lefty Richardson, editor of the Independent Record Company Magazine, wearing a T shirt which said 'Your Logo Here' and a leather jacket which said nothing, but looked uncomfortable, stepped forward to give tongue.

"It's wonderful to be here speaking on behalf of a wonderful industry which has gathered here tonight to honour its own wonderful talent. S'wonderful."

There was a feeling in the audience that Lefty had been drinking some wonderful Scotch before he climbed on stage.

"It has been a difficult choice - difficult choice. So much brilliant, I mean flabbergasting music has been made this year. Our industry can be proud - so proud."

The audience gave itself a huge round of applause and the evening slipped comfortably into the usual self congratulatory mode of all award ceremonies.

Half way through the proceedings Herbie ran into Josh at the bar. Happy as he had been before, he was even happier now.

"I'm so happy for you, recognition by the whole industry is not something to sneeze at. You know, I'm thinking on my feet now, but you should take advantage of this and maybe I can help. I mean what are friends for? I've got it, why don't I put out a new album from you guys? No, don't thank me. I feel I owe this band something."

"You do, about ten years back royalties."

"No! Stone me! I can hardly believe it. I mean it is all done by computer now-a-days, human error is literally cut to nothing. But if there has been some foul up in accounts, the million to one shot, I want to know why? I'm glad you mentioned this, Herbie, and don't worry, if there is a problem, it is as good as sorted." He paused while he grappled manfully with the possibility that his company had made an error. Then he continued: "That's it, debt of honour. We've got to do this album. Give us a ring." And picking up his drinks, he moved back to his table.

Colney Hatch were last on a very long list and by the time their turn came people were looking forward to stubbing out the fag end of the evening. Lefty gave an enthusiastic and rambling eulogy before peering hazily at the list in front of him and announcing, "Coley Hatch", thinking that the band must have something to do with fisheries. Nobody bothered to correct him.

"Twenty one thousand, that's seven thousand each, if you forget about what's his name and pay that other geezer session fees."

Joshua Marx leaned back in his chair and spread his hands in a 'can't say fairer than that' gesture. He was sitting with Colney Hatch at the back of his local pub having just treated the whole band to sandwiches and beer. He was offering them a single album deal with an option on a second if there was one and as usual he had pitched it just right. Seven thousand each was more than any of them could refuse and on paper it looked good. The reality wasn't quite as altruistic as it sounded.

They would be paying for the studio, most of the advertising and would have to give him the publishing. He would turn a nice little profit, while if they made one more penny out of the album his book keeping skills weren't what he thought they were.

"That sounds fine," said Herbie, "if we get the advance before we go into the studio."

He knew Josh, he could throw figures around like a man distributing confetti, but getting him to sign a cheque was like trying to raise the Titanic.

"When you want it, it is as good as in the bank. On my life. But if you take my advice you will hold off till after next April, to avoid tax problems. I'm only trying to do you a favour."

"Not a bad idea," said Herbie, "if you want the album next April? It's up to you."

"Or forget the whole thing," said Surrey, "I'm jammed up with work as it is."

"Yeah, right, and the school run doesn't get done by itself," muttered Screech.

"Alright, alright, the money's there. Now, when can you start recording?"

Benny was the Travesty Studio's engineer. He was small, baby faced, curly haired and grumpy. His expression was one continual sneer, which was his idea of a music business professional at work. The other members of the band were before his time, but he had worked with Herbie on the 'Killing the Blues' album, being primarily responsible for what had become charitably known as its 'authentically tinny sound'.

On the first day of recording the band clattered down into the basement with their instruments and pushed their way along the narrow corridor past the control room and into the studio. Benny was in there connecting up microphones and moving mic stands around with an air of sullen resignation. He ignored them all till the last possible moment.

"Hello Benny," said Herbie, "long time, no see." He indicated the others with a nod of his head. "Surrey, Screech, Bob. Bob is going to produce as well as play bass."

"Yeah?" Benny tried to smooth his sneer into a brief smile, but only achieved a horrible grimace, then he unbent to just this side of friendliness. "I'm sure we can get some great sounds," he muttered, "I've managed to get hold of an AC-1000-P-Burble processor on spec there is not much we can't do. The old one was crap."

"Sounds great," said Herbie, "but don't touch it. We like a natural sound."

Benny's pride and joy out of action before a shot had been fired. His mouth resumed its usual sulky down turn.

"Sort yourselves out," he said as he left the room, "I'm ready when you are."

"Anybody told him this is a studio, not a leper colony?" asked Surrey, taking his guitar from its case.

"He's worse once you get to know him," said Herbie.

"I don't intend to get to know him," said Screech, "Bob can get to know him and let me know how it goes."

They arranged themselves round the microphones and Benny's voice sneered metallically through the intercom: "O.K. check your tunings. What's this one called?"

"'Travelling Home'."

"'Rattling Bones'?"

"'Travelling' Home."

"Oh, 'Travelling Home'. God! That is so old hat. Never mind, we can change it later. O.K. 'Drivelling On' take one.'

Not surprisingly, Herbie fluffed a chord in the introduction and Benny's voice came through, almost cheery now, "I can fix that. Pick it up where you left off." The four of them drifted aimlessly on for another few bars before clattering to a halt.

"No problem," called Benny, insultingly dead pan. "Wait for it. 'Drivelling on' take two."

But Herbie had put down his guitar and taken out his rum flask. He treated himself to a good slug and then handed it round.

"Do you remember that engineer at Cambridge?" he said.

"The bloke who messed up our sound?" asked Surrey.

"That's the one." Herbie gave an almost imperceptible wink.

"Oh yeah," Screech laughed, "we super glued him to his mixing desk, then I accidentally hit him with a mic stand."

"They had to carry him into hospital still attached to it," chuckled Herbie.

"But it wasn't funny later," grinned Surrey, "he ended up with a phobia about touching electrical equipment and his teeth were never quite right afterwards."

"Still, it had to be done," sighed Herbie.

"True."

"Very true."

Benny, listening to this from the control room had been gripped by a vague sense of unease. This band seemed to have what could be called a robust sense of humour when it came to sound men and he wondered if he had been a shade too acerbic in his initial dealings. He got up and went into the recording area on the pretense of moving a microphone. As he pushed the sliding door, he was greeted by the sound of raucous laughter. No one noticed him as he came up behind Screech and said: "Everything alright, lads?"

Screech, who had just put the rum flask to his lips, swung round, his elbow catching Benny a glancing blow on the eye. There was a yelp of pain and Benny reeled back clutching his face.

"Watch where you're walking," joked Bob, "he uses that arm to play."

It did not go down well, Benny was convinced he had been the subject of a deliberate assault and no amount of apology by Screech could persuade him otherwise. He would have liked to cancel the session, but he knew that displays of temperament cut no ice with Josh. He bit the bullet and decided to play the wounded hero.

"I can make it," he said through gritted teeth, "the show must go on."

He went back into the control room and reset the tape.

"'Travelling on' take two," he announced primly, and the session flickered back to life.

By the end of the day they had four songs in the can and spirits soared.

"Back in the groove," yelled Screech, after hearing a re-run of the last take."

"The old firm," said Surrey.

"We're better than ever," said Herbie, "we ought to get back together and do the whole thing again."

"Right," the others chorused. They even went as far as to exchange a few high fives.

That was the crest and the resultant wave of good-will carried them through the next two days and four more tracks, then disaster struck.

Benny precipitated it by suggesting to Surrey that he add a chunky rhythm track to beef up the guitar part.

This was a mistake. A brilliant finger picking guitar player with a great tone, Surrey had never been able to master rhythm guitar, it took some sense of feel that he didn't have. But once the idea had been muted, he was too proud to back down and ask Herbie to do it. Instead, all eyes upon him from the control room, he sweated away trying to overdub chords that were becoming evermore inappropriately placed. Benny could not believe his luck, he had found a weakness and he leapt to exploit it mercilessly. At first he would let him get about halfway through the track before stopping the tape.

"Not quite on the money, I'm afraid. Better take it from the top."

The next phase was calling a halt almost immediately.

"No, still too ragged."

After that it became a war of attrition for about fifteen minutes until the final coup de grace.

"Sorry, my fault, I shouldn't have suggested it. We're not helping the track and we are getting bogged down. Let's move on."

Bob, who had not been taking much notice of Surrey's struggles, then told one of the time honoured jokes about drummers that musicians never seem to tire of and he and Screech and Herbie re-entered the recording area laughing. That was the last straw. Red faced and angry, lips compressed, beard bristling, Surrey could hardly wait for the first opportunity to strike back.

Herbie and Screech became aware of the change in atmosphere almost immediately. Years of playing together had made them all experts at recognizing each other's moods. Consequently, their own emotions ran quickly from innocent injury to angry resentment and the powder keg was ready to go. It only took a happily oblivious Bob to set the spark.

"How about Herbie and I laying down the vocals, guitar and bass on this one?" he said. "We could overdub the other guitar and violin, that way we would have more options when it came to the mixing. It's Surrey's turn to get the sandwiches, anyway."

"We could do that if Surrey and Screech fancy a break," said Herbie quickly, "I like a complete live take myself."

That put everything back in the open arena of discussion and probably would have resulted in a friendly decision one way or the other if Benny, listening from the control room, hadn't stuck his oar in.

"That's a great idea." The metallic, disembodied voice came over the system. "I'll have a crocodile sandwich and make it snappy, ha, ha, no, a cheese and pickle on brown, an orange juice and a packet of plain crisps."

"Wonderful," said Surrey, "suddenly I'm the boy, the flaming gofer. After twenty five years in the business."

"Not so suddenly," said Herbie, "everybody else has gone."

"Come on," said Screech, "I'll go with you. I need some fresh air."

Ten minutes later, Herbie and Bob and finished a take and looked round to the control room window to see if there had been any technical hitches. They were just in time to see the burly figure of Surrey taking a sandwich out of a paper back and grinding it into Benny's face. Then he took a packet of crisps, put it on the engineer's head and burst it open with an open palm. They didn't wait to see any more, they sprinted for the sliding doors.

Crashing into the control room, they saw a can of beer hit Screech on the head. Then pandemonium brook loose and it has to be said for Bob that, though only a temporary member of the band, he pitched in with as much vim and irresponsibility as the hardened campaigners.

It was at this point that Josh decided to stroll down and see how the recording was going. He had just sold one of his more useless artists to Warner Brothers for a good sum and was pleased with his morning's work. He opened the door at the bottom of the stairs into the basement and was suddenly aware of a confusion of sound and movement coming from the control room. If it wasn't some peculiar form of band therapy, a fight was going on.

He was shocked and annoyed. He hadn't expected much from this bunch of degenerates, but more than that. He was about to call a couple of hippie gnomes down to break it up when he saw the positive side. If the band broke anything, and they could hardly not in that confined space, they would have to pay for it and there were a few bits of equipment he would like to replace. He opened the door to the control room and looked around for a way to influence matters in his favour. His eye fell on the AC-1000-P-Burble. That old processor, he thought, it looks OK, but Benny said it was rubbish. I think we deserve a new one.

When the fight broke out, Benny, ignoring the indignity of the crisps and the sandwich, had slid quickly under the mixing desk. There he had received a few kicks, not all of them, he suspected, by accident. It was with relief that he saw Josh enter the room and he waited expectantly for the voice of authority to bring the battle to a close. But no. In frozen horror he saw Josh suddenly lean forward and rip his new AC-P-1000-Burble from the rack and raise it above his head. An agonized yell broke from his lips.

"Naaaah!

The fight stopped immediately and everybody spun round to see Josh smash the processor down on to the corner of an old Fender amp. A stunned silence ensued and Josh became uncomfortably aware of ten staring eyes.

"Now look what you've made me do," he said, "I've dropped our old processor."

"New processor," said Benny, "and it wasn't ours it was on spec."

"Well, I had to stop the fight somehow, didn't I? You weren't doing a lot. And who left this bloody amp here anyway? Come out from under that desk, for crying out loud. I'm trying to run a serious business here, you know what I mean, not a bleedin' kindergarten. All right, show's over, back to work." And he retreated with bad grace to his office.

Three days later they had the record in the can and Surrey and Screech had left to fulfil other commitments. Herbie and Bob were finishing up the mixing. Benny was being his usual obstructionist self.

"What do you mean there's echo on there? There is no echo, or very little."

"Take it off."

"I don't know if I can at this stage. It will make the studio sound flat."

"Take it off."

"OK if that's the sound you want, that's the sound you want and ten years engineering experience go for nothing. When I was working for the Sweet Dreams..."

"And this compression on the violin.."

"Now that absolutely makes the track."

"Can we try it without."

And so on, until they had arrived at a natural sound which pleased Bob and Herbie, but left Benny listlessly fiddling with knobs in a desultory attempt to show how lousy the whole thing sounded.

"Well that's a wrap," said Bob, when they had mixed the last track on to D.A.T. "as far as I'm concerned, we got a result."

"Damn right," grinned Herbie. "What do you say to a bottle of Champagne and a few sandwiches to celebrate." He pulled out a fifty quid note and threw it on to the mixing desk in front of Benny, "You're turn," he said.

"I'm not sure if I should leave the studio. Josh has this rule..."

"Don't worry about that, we'll cover for you. You're part of the team now. And you know the area better than we do."

"You're right," said Benny, "after all, what could go wrong?" And he prized himself loose from his chair and trotted upstairs.

As soon as he had gone, Herbie dropped the D.A.T. into his pocket while Bob spooled the last master tape from the machine and packed it into its box. Then he put it and the other two boxes of master tapes into a hold all. Three minutes later they were in the old Volvo heading for home.

"What, on my sainted aunt, are you playing at, Herbie?" asked Josh when he phoned up the next day. "You realize those tapes are my property and I would be perfectly justified in calling in the old bill, you know what I mean."

"I do know what you mean, Josh, and there is nothing to worry about. I just wanted to play the album to Mr. Mitchel-Fotheringay who is here with me now."

"Mitch? Your old bass player? Well, that is different. What has he been doing with himself all these years?"

"He qualified as a lawyer, specializing in Music Business Law."

"Oh."

"Yeah, he says that you're in breach of contract for non payment of royalties, so if you want to call in the police, it seems we can make a few counter claims. He thinks it could drag on for years and, as he has got an interest, he says he is prepared to work our side for nothing."

"After all I've done for you guys. I'll tell you, Herbie, frankly I'm disappointed. You know as well as I do that a small record company like mine isn't a business, it's an art form. It's all about the personal touch and looking out for the other fellow. We're not a big, cold conglomerate. Listen, bring the tapes back in and we'll talk."

"I'll bring the tapes in tomorrow, if you talk to Mitch today."

There was a long pause.

"OK Herbie, I'll see him at one o'clock this afternoon, if you can arrange it?"

"Of course I can arrange it," said Herbie, "after all, what are friends for?"

CHAPTER 8
TINKLING CYMBALS

You can't be a professional musician for very long without someone asking you to do a charity gig, which is what you'd expect in a society as charitable as our own. Everybody knows that entertainers live on air, so it is no trouble to them to play for free for a good cause. After all, they have the fun of living gay, glamorous lives, admired by all and sundry. Why shouldn't they be prepared to put something back occasionally? Anyway, most of them are so egotistical that you're doing them a favour to let them on any stage at all.

Herbie Watson did not subscribe to this view. He looked on charities as collections of hard nosed individuals whose main interest in fundraising was that it paid their own lucrative salaries and the pictures of dead seals, crippled children and starving farmers were valuable assets, the means by which they could reach this end. In theory he thought charity should be personal, you helped someone who needed it, you didn't pay someone else to do it, in practice he usually passed by on the other side. This pragmatic approach wasn't something he had dreamed up over night, it had been taught to him by years of bitter experience, so when Big John phoned him up with an offer of a great gig and a wonderful opportunity he was immediately on his guard.

"Hi ya Herbie, it's John, I'm back over from the States and looking to reciprocate for you getting me in at the Crossroads Club. It's a neat little charity gig that you're gonna just love."

"Big of you John, but it was nothing."

"No, no, you deserve it. Listen, it's these people down in Devon who have a place called Well Being House with lots of land. They bring in children from where ever the hell and give them a holiday. Of course, they also use it for fundraising and that's where we come in, you know, helping the little children."

"Well, that sounds wonderful, but I'm looking at my diary and I really can't see a window..."

"They own two or three other venues and they often promote Arts weekends and stuff. Once they know you, there's a little bit of a circuit there, not that that's a consideration."

"Of course not, not when there are little children to help, still, it's a pity I'm so full up. When is it anyway?"

"This weekend."

"This weekend? You mean the one coming?"

"That's what I said, this weekend."

"That is weird, man, it must have been meant to happen. Do you know that by some miracle this weekend is clear."

"Well, wadda you know! So you'll do it?"

"You've twisted my arm. How do we get there?"

"I've been let down on some transport, so we'll have to go in your car. Of course, I'll share the driving, if I can remember which side of the road I'm supposed to be on."

Big John arrived at Herbie's place at ten o' clock on Saturday morning. They put their guitars in the back of the Volvo and headed off.

"You know, Herbie," said Big John, "after an hour's lecture on how to fry a steak, "these people love me down there, they've made me an angel."

"What do they want you to do, back a show?"

"No, it's a real accolade. I helped them out a bit, you know how it is, I'm a sucker for a good cause and they put me on their list of special donors."

"I wouldn't mind a coffee, shall we stop at the next services?"

"Sure. You know, when you see what a good job these folks are doing, you might want to become an angel too."

"Not a bad idea, and then maybe they would give me a percentage if I introduced other donors."

"Boy, I could sure use that coffee."

Well Being House was a gaunt, Victorian building set in run down grounds miles from anywhere. There were two expensive people carriers parked in the front drive and wind chimes hanging over the door. Herbie came out of the lane too fast, jerked on the brakes and came to a halt in a cloud of dust, missing one of the people carriers by inches. They both got out and stretched to ease their stiff muscles. Herbie started to roll a cigarette.

"Well, here we are," said Big John, taking a deep breath and looking expansively round, "ain't you glad you came?"

"NO SMOKING!" A shrill, high pitched voice shattered the stillness. They spun round and saw a sharp faced girl with red, frizzy hair wearing what looked like a sack for a dress coming towards them. Herbie frowned down at her as he dug out his lighter from his pocket.

"Ssh! You'll wake the baby," he said, lighting up.

The girl stopped in her tracks and peered towards the car.

"What baby?" she whispered.

"Any baby within ten miles. Now, what's the problem?"

Her voice hardened.

"We have a no smoking policy throughout Well Being."

Big John stepped forward.

"Now, hold on there, er Cruella ..."

"The name's Katie."

"Right, Katie, I think the Earth Mother means inside the house. I'm a non smoker myself, but he can't do a bit of harm out here and this boy's come along way to help you folks."

Katie, mollified by Big John's Southern charm, gradually recovered from her spasm and re-entered the real world.

"I'll ask Mrs Thornbury, I expect it will be all right as long as he stays in the garden. Actually, I thought he was coming into the house."

"No, siree, we're just relaxing after the long drive. When's supper?"

"Dinner is is at seven o'clock. Come in when you're ready and I'll show you where you're going to play."

Inside, the house was dark and somnambulant, with the atmosphere of a small country hotel run by funeral directors. The hall had a polished wood floor with rugs, a settee, one or two chairs and a door leading to an office. Outside the office was a table with leaflets and a few CDs on it, Big John's and, Herbie noted with surprise, some of his own. He looked questioningly at Big John.

"I happened to have a few left over, so I thought I'd spread the light,"

They knocked on the door of the office and waited. Nothing. They tried again. Still nothing.

"Yodleedeeodeadee!" sang Herbie into the silence.

"Shushhh!" A sound like rapidly stir fried vegetables came from the top of the stairs to be followed by a large round faced woman with long grey hair and black eyebrows. She wore a free flowing dark green dress with a yellow stone on a leather necklace around her neck.

"The Earth Mother," muttered Big John. "Hi ya June," he called, "let me introduce you to my good friend Herbie Watson."

She held out a regal hand.

"June Thornbury, Mr Watson, I'm the House Mother at Well Being. I must ask you not to make too much noise, we have meditation sessions going on at the moment."

"Sorry," said Herbie, "but Katie was going to show us where we are going to play and she seems to have disappeared."

The House Mother tut tutted and for a moment it looked as if she was going to yell out for her errant acolyte then, glancing at Herbie, she recollected herself.

"I'll show you," she sighed.

She took them across the hall to a large room with tables lined along the walls in preparation for the evening buffet. There were a few chairs and a French window leading out to a veranda. At one end of the room over an unlit fireplace was a large painting of some Indian musicians sitting on cushions in an ornate palace.

"You will play there," she said waving towards it, "after the sitar recital. Now, you will no doubt want to rest. You are staying in the guest cottage on the left hand side of the drive. I will get the keys from the office."

Two hours later, after a rest and a wash, Herbie was making coffee in the kitchen of the cottage.

"So," he was saying, "where are all the little children?"

Big John was opening and shutting cupboards looking for food.

"They get about two weeks a year and a lot of publicity. The last guests here must have been locusts - not a thing."

Herbie poured out the coffee.

"It's nice to know that while we are giving up our time and working for nothing that these people are getting something out of it. A nice house to live in and no children to bother them."

"Negative, Herbie, too negative. The organization is a mite top heavy, I'll give you that, but at least the kids get two weeks. Anyway, the way I look at it is, the kids are working for them as much as they are working for the kids. You can live off failure just as well as you can live off success in this man's society. Now let's go over and see what they've got for eats."

Supper was saffron rice, an anaemic vegetable Curry and chapatis. The attractions of Well Being House obviously did not include cordon bleu cookery. The guests milled about eating off paper plates, looking relaxed and casual in short sleeved shirts and jeans. You could see the calm confidence of super solvency behind their friendly smiling eyes. Katie introduced them to a big bearded man with a pair of half glasses tied to his neck with a red cord, telling them he was going to give a short lecture before the music. Neither of them was listening closely enough to find out what it was going to be about. Herbie took a chapati and went out through the open French window away from the crowd. Big John grabbed two chapatis and followed him. They were both annoyed at being expected to eat with the audience before a show. It was bad for business, even if there was no business.

"Boy, these guys freeze on to a dollar. What do they think we are, a bunch of photographer's models?"

"Yeah" said Herbie broodingly, finishing his chapati and lighting a cigarette. "Do you want to go on first?"

"Sure, no, wait a minute, I'd better close the show as I'm featured in the advertising. You know how important that sort of thing is to these folks."

"Of course."

The sitar player and a tabla player dressed in full Indian regalia came out of the shadows and joined them.

"Have they finished eating?" asked the sitar player, "we're due on at eight."

"No," said Herbie, "there's some guy going to give a spiel first. Cigarette?"

They both rolled up and Herbie asked them what part of India they were from.

"Tooting, South London," they grinned, "but don't mention it, they think we're straight from New Delhi."

When Katie came out to tell them that the lecture was over and they were ready for them to go on, they gave her a small brass jar with two joss sticks in it and a box of matches.

"Put centre stage, makee light," said the sitar player, whose English had suddenly taken a down turn, "good Karma."

A few moments later they made their way on stage exuding the mysticism of the East.

After the gig the four musicians sat out on the veranda and shared a few bottles of wine bought from Well Being House at an outrageous mark up. Their theory was you shouldn't have been drinking in the first place, but if you were going to it was only right to overcharge because it was for charity.

It was a warm summer evening and the lights from the dining room window and the open French window made patches of warm colour on the veranda. They sat at a wrought iron table at one end and smoked and passed the bottle, all except Big John who clutched a mineral water in his meaty hand. Gradually, the sounds in the house died down and, when Katie came out to close the French window and switch out the lights, there were three empty bottles on the table and one doing the rounds. Sajit, the sitar player, was talking about studying music in India and how the art was passed down in families.

"You never know," said Herbie, "that painting in there of musicians playing in what looks like a Rajah's palace might be some of your ancestors."

"Yeah, that's funny," Mogul, the tabla player, said, "Sajit and I were talking about it earlier, that painting is worth a lot of money."

"Really?" Big John tilted his chair forward and leaned his elbows on the table.

"Yes, I think it was done by a famous Indian artist called Rajit Singh, late eighteenth century. It was probably left here by the family that once owned this house. They obviously had no idea what it was worth."

By the time they got back to the cottage Herbie had had a bottle and a half of wine on an empty stomach, and he was feeling it.

"God, I'm hungry," he said. "Where can we get hold of some food?"

"At this time of night, nowhere. We've got one more show to do in the morning then I'm gonna head for the nearest road stop and I'm gonna buy you... we can buy ourselves the biggest plate of ham and eggs you ever saw."

"Right, but that's way in the future, what about now? I'm going to look for the kitchen. They should all be asleep and those French windows would give with a push."

"Hold on, Herbie, that's the wine talking, breaking and entering is not a good idea."

"Maybe not, but they owe us something."

"If that's the way you feel, bring back a slice of ham."

"O.K. you get the coffee going, I won't be long."

Outside there was a full moon and not a cloud in the sky. The garden glowed with a silver light. Herbie walked to the house and round to the veranda. He didn't anticipate any trouble, his only worry was whether there would be any real food to steal. What he had seen so far gave him cause for concern. He crept up to the French windows and pushed, they didn't give. Then he remembered that they opened outwards. He tried pulling. There was a disturbingly loud rattle, but the doors remained resolutely closed. It looked as if he would have to break the glass and that didn't seem like the quietest way to enter a house at two o'clock in the morning. He had started to sober up and was beginning to regret his decision to break in. He was turning to step back off the veranda when something caught his eye. He spun back again. Yes, he had been right, some-one had left one of the windows open. That changed everything, a child could do it now. He gently raised the window a few inches more and swinging his leg through, he ducked into the room.

At first he couldn't see a thing, very little moonlight filtered into the room because of the overhang on the veranda. Cautiously he moved forward, hands waving in front of him, eventually he bumped into one of the tables lined against the opposite wall. Now he knew where he was. He felt his way along and reached the door. He opened it and slid into the hall. He was begin-ning to distinguish shapes, darker and less dark. Over by the fireplace there was a glimmer of moonlight. The kitchen was through a passageway on one side of the of-fice. He made it, meeting nothing worse than a couple of creaking boards, which made him pause, but noth-ing stirred.

The kitchen was a large room with a big wooden table in the centre and the sink, cooker, fridge and cup-boards around the walls. Again, there were no curtains on the windows. It must be the result of some moon fe-tish, thought Herbie, they probably all take moon baths and run about naked in thistle strewn fields. Spotting the white door of the fridge he opened it and was mo-mentarily blinded by an explosion of light. As his eyes adjusted they fell on a plate of ham that hadn't got as far as the guests. He wrapped it up in a piece of kitchen towel and tucked it into his jean jacket along with a half pound of butter and a loaf of bread. Then he closed the fridge door and retreated.

By the time he got back to the dining room his eyes seemed to be more accustomed to the gloom. Maybe the moon had moved round creating fractionally more light. He had crossed to the opposite wall and was ducking through the open window onto the veranda when he suddenly had the feeling that something was wrong. He looked carefully around. Then he saw what it was. The painting had gone. The whiteness of the blank space seemed to glow in the darkness. Burglary. He went through the window like a scalded cat and vanished silently into the protective darkness of the grounds. When he got back to the cottage Big John was sitting in the kitchen in front of a steaming pot of coffee.

"Someone's half inched the painting," said Herbie.

"We want food, not an art retrospective. What did you get?"

Herbie retrieved the ham, butter and bread from his jacket and laid them on the table. They got out knives and plates and were soon biting into ham sandwiches washed down by mugs of black coffee. After they had eaten three each in silence, Herbie tried again.

"On my way through the dining room, I noticed that the painting wasn't there. It's been stolen. That is why the window was open when I arrived."

"What? Why didn't you say so?" Big John mumbled through a full mouth. "We gotta act fast. There ought to be a finders fee if we save the insurance company a pay out and it can't have gone very far." He reached for another sandwich.

"There are only two people it could be," said Herbie, "Sajit and Mogul, they knew the value of the painting and they probably have contacts that could get it out of the country and sell it in India."

"Right, we have to tackle them now, they won't be expecting anybody to confront them so soon."

Sajit and Mogul were staying in a camper van parked near the house. It was three o'clock in the morning and, what with the long drive, the gig and the wine, they were sleeping more than the sleep of the just, they were totally flat out. It hadn't occurred to either of them to lock the door, so there was no warning. From out of nowhere two big, black, burly, self righteous shapes were suddenly shaking them into wakefulness. If they hadn't led such blameless lives they would have been reminded of a police raid, as it was they were reminded of horror films with axe murderers and vengeful zombies.

"Hey!" said an American voice which in the circumstances was strangely reminiscent of Jack Nicholson's, "are you guys awake?"

They were awake all right.

Herbie had found the light switch and the camper was flooded with light. Instead of axe murderers they saw two folk musicians. It was a tough call, but on balance they preferred folk musicians.

"Forget it, fellows," said Sajit, "the evening is over." He looked at his watch. "It's three in the morning, the wine has gone, now it's time for sleep. Switch off the light on your way out."

"Where's the painting?" said Big John.

'Do yourselves a favour," said Herbie, "if we put it back now, no one will be any the wiser."

Big John saw his finders fee fading into the distance.

"At least we can negotiate," he said.

"What the hell are you talking about?" asked Mogul.

Ten minutes later everything was clear, Sajit and Mogul did not have the painting; but if they didn't have it who had? Naturally, it didn't take long for men of their calibre to work that out.

The open window was just a blind. There wasn't time after they had left the veranda for anyone to break in, steal the painting and get away without being seen by Herbie on his way back to the house. Sajit and Mogul had seen a gipsy encampment near by yesterday and it was an obvious attempt to lay the blame on them. If so, then it had to be somebody inside the house. It was unlikely to be one of the guests, as people did not usually go to expensive meditation week-ends with the intention of getting away with the silver. So, who was it? For a moment it looked as if the investigation was going to peter out.

Suddenly, Sajit remembered the dodgy bloke with the beard and it all became clear. The lecturer, it was a natch. But where had he hidden it? Not in his room, too risky. Not in the grounds, it might rain and also very difficult to retrieve without being seen. That left his car. He must have waited until Katie had locked up and put out the lights. Then, while they were talking on the veranda, he had taken the painting out the front door and put it in his car. Of course! and tomorrow, once the police and everybody had gone off chasing gipsies, he would drive quietly and innocently away.

All they had to do was to take it out of his car and hide it in the cottage. Then in the morning, after it had been declared stolen, don't forget the finder's fee, they would hand it back, revealing all.

Breaking into the lecturer's car turned out to be easy. It was an old Morris Traveller, so Sajit, who was a mechanic in his spare time, was able to open the driver's side door with a wire coat hanger. In the back, wrapped in cloth and plastic sheeting, was the painting. Eureka! They unlocked the back doors, slid the painting out, re-arranged the cloth and re-locked them again to make it look as if nothing had been disturbed. Retreating into the night, they congratulated each other on a brilliant piece of detective work and separated to indulge in some well earned rest.

Breakfast was fruit juice, rolls and coffee, or tea, served between eight and nine in the dining room. Herbie and Big John just made it for nine. Two tables were joined together in the centre of the room with chairs and places set on either side. Half a dozen guests were lingering over their coffee and chatting. The space above the fireplace looked glaringly empty. On their way into breakfast they had noticed that the Morris Traveller had gone, the bearded bloke was probably half way to London by now. They exchanged self-satisfied grins and sat down to eat.

A couple of people congratulated them on their performances the night before and asked them if they were playing again. They told them they were due on at eleven o'clock and. after polite expressions of anticipation, the conversation drifted into other channels. No one mentioned the painting. Surely, thought Herbie, that was odd, or were these people so blasé that a burglary in someone else's house was a matter of complete indifference to them? Finally, Big John couldn't stand the suspense any longer. He selected his nearest neighbour.

"What happened to the painting, bud?"

"Of course, you missed Professor Jones's lecture. It seems to be quite an important work. Evidently, they agreed to lend it to him for an exhibition in Bristol in exchange for his talk last night."

Herbie stood up.

"Come on, John, we'd better be getting ready for the gig."

"Sure, we'll see you folks later.

They ambled out of the dinning room and through the hall, breaking into a run as they reached the front door. Five minutes later they had packed, loaded up the Volvo and were ready to go.

"Hold on," said Big John, "I gotta see the Earth Mother about the CD.s."

He disappeared inside the house to re-emerge a few moments later holding a wad of tens.

"I thought you had donated those," said Herbie.

"Well, kind of, they sell them for £15, I get £10 they get £5."

"To give to the little children."

"Sure, whatever. Let's go."

As Herbie reversed the car round in a cloud of dust Mrs Thornbury fluttered out of the front door towards them.

"Mr Tucker, Mr Watson, are you leaving? I thought you were going to play for us again."

Big John leaned out the window.

"Sorry, Ma'am, urgent call from London. But we want to make it up to you, so we left a donation in the cottage."

"That sounds wonderful," said Mrs Thornbury.

"He who has not charity is but a tinkling cymbal," said Herbie, sententiously. And, with a cheerful wave, they roared off down the drive.

CHAPTER 9

THE KING OF CAMDEN

The gig had not gone well and, as the ten or twelve customers filed out of the darkened room, Herbie Watson stood at the back of the club trying to salvage something from the wreckage by selling a few copies of his 'Killing the Blues' CD. This, he was musing bitterly, is what happens when a club organizer can't be bothered to get his act together. As he was always telling his agent and his agent was always telling him, without, it has to be said, any noticeable affect on either of them, there are three ways to make a gig successful, Promotion, Promotion, Promotion. He remembered reading somewhere that when Elvis played Las Vegas Colonel Parker told him that even the gophers in the desert would know about it. Herbie wasn't sure if there were any gophers around Nottingham, but, if there were, they certainly hadn't heard about this gig.

A balding, quiet man in glasses and a duffel coat sidled up beside him. Herbie cranked a grim smile up on to his face and growled a hello.

"My name is Edmund Edmunds," said the man, "and I am now managing Amos Elliot."

"That's great, Eddie."

"Edmund."

"Pleased to hear it, Edmund. How is Amos these days? Would you like a copy of my 'Killing the Blues' CD? I know Amos would love to hear it."

"That's very kind of you."

"No trouble at all," said Herbie handing it to him, "ten pounds."

"Oh, I thought you were giving it to me. Maybe I'd better..."

"Why on earth would I give you, a complete stranger, valuable merchandise? This is a business, if you are not interested, move along and make room for somebody who is."

"No, no, I'll take it. I want to talk to you anyway."

There was a slight twinkle in Herbie's eyes as he placed the tenner in his wallet alongside his night's earnings.

"I've been trying to persuade Amos to get back into doing some gigs," continued Edmund, shoving the CD into a coat pocket. "I know you were greatly influenced by him musically and I wondered if you would like to do something with him, you know, a sort of welcome back concert. I think I can guarantee that it will be a prestigious event and one that you really ought to be involved in."

"That's wonderful. You're right, Amos's music meant a lot to me when I was a young... er younger." He pulled a card out of his shirt pocket and handed it to him "That's my agent. Sort it out with him, I never discuss money."

But Edmund was not to be put off so easily.

"Thanks," he said, "I thought you would be interested, but if I phoned your agent to discuss money, we wouldn't be talking very long because there is no fee, of course you would get a percentage of the door money - after expenses."

Herbie's eyes glazed over. "Oh, that kind of prestigious," he said.

"Well, a lot of promoters won't touch him because of his record, you know how it is."

Herbie did know how it was and how it had been for a long time. His mind drifted back to the old days.

Amos Elliot had been a glitteringly successful musician until marijuana, heroin, speed and egotism had pushed his already fragile mentality over the edge into psychosis. Tall and strong with the looks and bearing of an army officer, he had towered over the London folk scene of the mid Sixties like a Zulu over Pygmies. Other musicians had admired his eccentric style, copied his technique and learned his instrumentals. It was considered a badge of excellence among rival guitarists to be able to play his tune, 'Senorita'.

Herbie too had studied his records, learned his tunings and spent many a self satisfied hour lamenting his demise with other musicians and wondering how it was that he had never made the big time. Guitarists he had influenced and who had gone on to become more famous tended to shake their heads knowingly whenever the subject came up. They felt that he had always been too real, too street, almost too big to become big and maybe they were right.

But being close to a genius was not close enough for Amos. Fuelled by drugs his inner imbalance and insecurities came out and he suffered a series of mental breakdowns, an Icarus who had flown too close to the sun of his own personality. To protect him from reality, doctors blithely put him on medication designed to raise a woolly wall between himself and the world. At the same time this also had the effect of protecting the world from him by placing him not in a padded cell, but in a padded mind.

When he came to, Edmund was still burbling on, Herbie immediately interrupted him.

"Listen, mate, nice talking to you, but I've got to go. Ring my agent and let him know what you've got planned, if I can do it I will." He closed the CD box and picked up his guitar.

"Maybe you wouldn't mind giving me a lift," said Edmund, "I think I've missed the last train.

"I'm sorry, I live in London, I don't know Nottingham at all and I am in a bit of a rush to get back because I'm expecting a phone call from the States."

"But I'm going to London as well. I was only up here visiting my sister. And the cat, I didn't leave her much food, she might be..."

Herbie gave up. "All right," he said, "come on."

The journey was a nightmare. Normally, Herbie trucked back along the near deserted motorways composing a song or a tune in his head, or recalling some imperfect scene from his past which he would replay in his mind, this time getting the starring roll with all the best punch lines. He never lost concentration and he never felt sleepy.

Tonight it was different, Edmund never stopped talking, his voice low and insistent. He started off talking about the music he liked, which players, which CDs, even which tracks. Herbie tried to stay with him by making the occasional polite grunt, enough to show he was listening, but hopefully not enough to encourage him. It didn't work. He was encouraged. He went on to describe his childhood illnesses, his marriage, his divorce and so on and so forth, but Herbie could have told you nothing about any of it. Everything had merged into a blurred hum and all he knew was that he was engaged in a life and death struggle against sleep.

He opened the window and sucked in deep lung fulls of motorway air, lowering the temperature in the car to freezing point. He rolled and lit cigarettes. He turned the radio on and off a few times, but that was just more chatter interspersed with musical drivel. The only thing he didn't do was pull off the motorway and have a coffee, he was damned if he was going to have one more minute of Edmund's company than absolutely necessary.

It wasn't until they were coming into London that Edmund said something which penetrated Herbie's consciousness. He was vaguely aware that the words Wandsworth Prison had floated into to the atmosphere and he shifted in his seat uncomfortably. What was this, an embarrassing confession, or had Edmund's father been a hangman, or something? He stared blankly ahead and waited to be unimpressed.

"They said I took the money, but I never did. Anyway, it was only five hundred out of petty cash. I'd have paid it back. It was for my mother..."

"What did you get?" interrupted Herbie.

"Three months, the judge had it in for me, but the worst of it was they wouldn't take me back at the betting shop."

"Tough."

"It worked out all right, if it wasn't for that I wouldn't be doing this for Amos."

"There you go," said Herbie, dismissing the story as pure fantasy. He had long since given up trying to work out why people talked bullshit most of the time. A little while later he dropped him off in Chiswick and put the whole incident out of his mind.

Two weeks later his list of gigs for the following two months came through from his agent, late as usual. Most of the work came in small groupings of three or four gigs in a row with the occasional dead header in between. It was not a heavy schedule, but it looked like enough to keep him going through December and even into January. He tossed the list on to the coffee table and got up to pour himself a drink. Then he picked up his map of England and a pencil and sat down again on the sofa. He took a sip of rum, sighed with satisfaction and pulled the list towards him. This was the closest he got to feeling like a business man and he enjoyed it. All he had to do was work out which gigs he had to stay out on the road for and which ones he could get home from, then he would arrange accommodation.

He quietly perused the list for a while, occasionally making marks with the pencil. Suddenly he let out a strangled cry, dropped the pencil, grabbed his glass and took a large gulp. A line of words, full of sinister import had caught his eye.

13 December: Cecil Sharpe House, London, with Amos Elliot. Fee: Fifty percent of the door to be split with Amos Elliot.

Twenty five percent of the take to play with a man who was as likely to be practicing his knife throwing in the dressing room as he was to be changing his guitar strings, if, in fact, he remembered to bring a guitar. What was his agent playing at? He leapt for the phone.

His agent lived in a small village on the Suffolk/ Norfolk border and did most of his business from the local pub. That meant phoning his mobile which Herbie rarely did. Cursing the expense he picked up the receiver and dialled the number.

"Hey, Alvin, it's Herbie."

"Arr, 'erbie, all right, boy? You got the list I expect, I done you proud this time."

"Aces, Alvin, aces, I'll be earning a living next, but that's what I'm calling you about, what's this charade with Amos Elliot?

"Arr, nice of you 'erbie, I don't expect the commission will be much. I don't mind just this once, but don't make a habit of it, boy."

Herbie began to smell a rat and he was pretty sure he knew its name.

"You've been talking to Edmund Edmunds," he said, "what did he tell you?"

"He told me you had agreed to do a gig with your old hero Amos Elliot, any time, any place, any fee.

Knowing you as I do, I was surprised, but he assured me it was true. Anyway, I expect this lad is popular, you should do all right." Alvin knew nothing and cared less about English folk music, he liked Classic Jazz, full stop.

"Are you kidding," exploded Herbie, "I'm the big draw, Amos is of purely historic interest, we'll be lucky if he even turns up for the gig.."

"He will," said Alvin, "Edmund has arranged for you to pick him up and take him, but you can work all that out between you at the rehearsal."

'Rehearsal', the word ground in Herbie's ear like a key in a rusty lock. His mind reeled as he grappled with the concept. It was against his whole artistic credo, work without payment.

"Oh, I don't think we need go as far as that," he said hoarsely.

"The 10th of December at two o' clock," said Alvin, "someone is supposed to be filming the concert for television. Don't let me down, Herbie, this could grow green."

Camden used to be the 'street life' centre of London, but that was when people thought of it as a run down area full of faded, smoke filled pubs inhabited by lonely Irishmen. Now-a-days it is just playing the part and has become a tourist trap and posers paradise.

Amos Elliot lived away from the bustle in a quiet street near the railway line, a leafy lane in summer where children played and traffic wardens strolled. Today the trees were bare, standing stark and cold in the chill grey afternoon, the children were away throwing shopping trolleys into the canal and only one traffic warden was left to watch morosely as Herbie parked his car. He took his guitar from the back seat, filled the meter full of coins and went up the steps to the front door. At least, he thought, as he rang the bell, the meter limits the rehearsal to two hours.

Amos Elliot opened the door looking calm and austere. He was wearing a perfectly fitting suede jacket, shirt and tie. His light brown curly hair was cut short round the head.

"Ah, Herbert, long time no see, muchacho, come in and let's get the road on the show." He turned and led the way into the flat making Donald Duck noises.

Herbie picked up his guitar case and followed him into the front room, a place of joss sticks, rugs and dark wooden furniture. A guitar and a mandolin hung on one wall. Herbie was glancing over at the instruments when something whizzed past his ear and he heard a thud behind him. Turning round he saw a knife embedded in a dart board fixed to the back of the door. He swung back to see Amos studying him with a faint smile on his face."

"I don't do much knife throwing these days," said Amos, "when you can split a match box nine times out of ten it becomes boring."

"I can well believe that," said Herbie, "I'm bored already. Come on, get your guitar and let's play."

This brought a sour note to the proceedings. Amos didn't like Herbie's tone, he expected deference at all times. He reached down his guitar in stoney silence. Perching majestically on a stool, he waved his hand at a smaller one in front of him and hit a couple of out of tune chords, glaring straight at Herbie, as if defying him to mention it.

"Do you know Spanish Blues?" he asked.

"Know it," said Herbie," I wrote it.

"No, I wrote it, you stole it."

"Rubbish, I nicked a few of the runs from Lightening Hopkins, the rest could more or less be said to be my own."

"And what about the Moorish influence, lifted straight from my Sheikh da Musik."

"Oh, so you own Morocco now, well, stone me!"

The two stared at each other for a moment, then Herbie pulled himself together.

"Wait a minute, we'll get nowhere if we carry on like this, you play something and I'll see what I can do."

Amos started off with "Junkie Blues". It wasn't bad. Apart from a few fumbled runs, the elements of the old blues shouter were still there and Herbie was more or less able to stay on board. But almost immediately things started to disintegrate and he watched in horror as it became apparent that he was witnessing the forlorn meanderings of a lost soul clutching desperately at wisps of talent and technique that medication had put forever beyond his grasp.

The strange thing was that there was a musical mind still at work. He would play a Balkan tune or a set of Greek dances and it would sound like a child thrashing a guitar he didn't know how to play. But beneath the rattlings, splutterings and half achieved melodies, Herbie could still make out some of the ideas Amos was hearing in his head. It was like trying to follow a conversation in a language of which you only know a few words.

Through it all Amos never acknowledged a mistake or showed the slightest embarrassment, in fact, he seemed more impatient with Herbie's attempts at accompaniment than at anything he was doing himself. Eventually they both ground to a halt.

"Well, I think that about covers it," said Amos, "but you must brush up on the Greek tunes. I'll expect you to have all these numbers at your finger tips by the day of the concert."

"I think I'll leave the Greek tunes to you." said Herbie, "they're a bit too esoteric for me."

The day of the concert rolled around and the first thing Herbie knew of it was when the phone rang at seven o'clock in the morning. He groggily picked up the receiver and heard Amos' voice floating down the line sounding like the caterpillar in 'Alice in Wonderland'.

"Morning, Herbie, fancy sharing a bottle of whisky with me?"

It was obvious that he had been up all night on God knows what and, if the gig was going to take place, he had to be stopped before oblivion set in. Herbie went into overdrive.

"I'm coming straight over," he said, "don't start without me."

He was out of bed and into a shirt and a pair of jeans in ten seconds flat. He pulled on his boots and stumbled into the bathroom to plunge his face in cold water. Then sinking half a pint of milk to line the stomach, he grabbed his jacket and guitar and was out the door, cursing Edmund Edmunds, his agent, Amos Elliot and anyone else he could think of.

When he got there he found Amos sitting at a low table with a couple of Camden dead beats passing a joint back and forth. The whisky was in the middle of the table - unopened.

While Amos was out of the room getting the glasses, Herbie explained to the two dead beats that the great man had an important gig that evening and it was up to the three of them to keep him sober. Amidst an odd selection of twitches and conspiratorial nods and winks, they agreed to help. Never before had getting more wasted than the next man been a duty, a way of making a contribution to art and society and now that the call had come they would not be found wanting.

Amos was already too spaced to notice that the game had been rigged. While he discoursed aimlessly on clouds, carpets, women, and Peruvian pan pipes, the dead beats splashed whisky into his glass and funnelled it into their own, rolled huge joints which somehow hardly ever reached him and clandestinely sniffed some stuff that seemed to have no other purpose than to sand blast the brain. Herbie pitched in as well and was soon following the thread of Amos's conversation with no problem at all.

As the day wore on and he wore out Herbie saw that there was an unspoken camaraderie between the three born of shared dissipation. Amos was the leader because he was or had been famous, but the other two were only acolytes because they wanted to possess him. He gave a cachet to their life story, with him they were part of an inner ring, without him they were no more than bleary, red eyed drunks sharing a cider bottle on a park bench.

When the time finally came to go to the gig, Amos changed into a dinner suit with a necklace of Indian beads draped across his gleaming white shirt front. He looked as fresh as a daisy, unlike Herbie who felt as ragged as an out of condition boxer after losing a fight. They left the flat and while the two dead beats retreated to some wilderness of their own, the stars clambered into the Volvo and negotiated the half mile to Cecil Sharpe House, the headquarters of the English Folk Song and Dance Society.

Edmund Edmunds was in the main hall where the gig was to take place watching the P.A. and lights being set up. He ignored Herbie and greeted Amos effusively who walked right past him and up on to the stage where he started banging on a piano and laughing to himself.

"Why are you doing this, Edmund?" asked Herbie, after watching the antics on stage for a long minute.

"I'm a lonely, no account bum, strangely awash with self satisfaction who is out of a job and therefore has time on his hands. I have always wanted to be thought of as important and Amos's vulnerability gave me the opportunity. I determinedly don't see the man standing in front of me, but cling to my memory of the star from yesteryear. Also, I'd like to make some easy money."

That is what he should have said, what he actually said was: "I wanted to do something for Amos, I think it is a crying shame the way he has been ignored all these years."

"He's not up to it," said Herbie.

"Oh, he'll be all right," said Edmund, complacently, "anyway, the hall is sold out."

"What!"

"Certainly, the interest in Amos... and yourself is such that I hardly had to do any promotion at all."

The TV crew turned up, swathed in scarves, short leather jackets and woollen hats. They went to work under the assumption that nothing else was happening, or could happen unless they gave it life by filming it. Cameras, light meters and tripods, barely controlled by their keepers, rampaged round the room while an extremely young looking director worked on his Cecil B. DeMille impression..

"This lot with an independent production company?" asked Herbie, as he watched Edmund arranging the float in the petty cash tin.

"No," said Edmund, "they're film students. I told them that I was in the process of selling an idea for a programme about Amos to Channel Four. I think it adds to the atmosphere, don't you?"

"If you say so," said Herbie, "I'd better go and do my sound check."

He had hardly finished before the crowds started filing in. As he watched, a warm wave of appreciation for Edmund and Amos rolled over him. The hall held about three hundred. At £10 a ticket that made a total of £3,000. Expenses and Edmund could hardly take more than £2,000, which left £1,000 to be split between him and Amos. These days £500 was pretty good for a night's work. He decided to be generous and offer Edmund a lift home. He strolled down to the door where the promoter was collecting money hand over fist.

"I'll drop you back after the show, if you like," he muttered.

"Thanks, Herbie, but no thanks, I've got the Volkswagen with me. Good evening, sir, that will be £10, please."

"OK" said Herbie, "I'm going outside for a cigarette."

It was a gusty evening with a chill in the air. People were still arriving in a steady stream, so he moved away from the entrance, lit a cigarette and stared up at some trees near the artist's parking area. This guy Edmunds is all right, he thought, he may be a bit of a bore, but he certainly knows how to organize a concert, or maybe it was just beginners luck. Either way he wouldn't mind working with him again and he didn't even have to drive him home. He laughed to himself as he remembered the journey back from Nottingham; if promoting didn't work, Edmund could certainly get a job curing insomniacs. He took a final drag on his cigarette, threw it into some bushes and turned to go back inside. Suddenly, he stopped. Prison. Why had that word come into his mind? What was the connection? He had been thinking about Edmund Edmunds - that was it - Wandsworth Prison, Edmunds had been in it - for stealing. He turned back and stared at the three cars and two vans parked nearby. There it was, the Volkswagen, solid and silent in the darkness. Herbie looked at it musingly.

He was standing at the side of the stage ready to go on when a man with a camera on his shoulder grooved alongside.

"Hey, Mr Watson, I'm going to be moving around during your set to get a few angles and supplementary shots to back up Tarquin on the main camera, just ignore us and play your normal gig."

"OK" said Herbie, "by-the-way have you got permission to foul up the audience's evening like this?"

"Well, Mr Edmunds..."

"He's only speaking for Amos Elliot, if you want to film me you have to get clearance at the highest level."

"Who's that?"

"Me."

"Can we..."

"No." And he ambled on stage to a roar of applause, half of which was from people who thought he was the legendary Amos Elliot.

At half time the buzz was almost tangible, the famous recluse, the old master, the guitar picker's guitar picker was about to take the stage. Would he be able to recapture past glories, or would it be another case of 'over the hill'? Amos, resplendent in his dinner suit and Indian beads gave no hint of the cacophony to come. He gazed imperiously around, lord of all he surveyed, and what he surveyed was pay dirt. All he had to do was make sure the mask didn't slip for an instant.

Herbie watched from the back as Amos went into his act. The first few numbers were all right, the audience subdued by his austere persona. Then he started in on the Greek tunes. Still he was listened to, after all, maybe he was into Schoenburg now. But as the flounderings continued the truth began to dawn on even the most unmusical minds. Something was wrong.

At this point Herbie turned to look at the ticket desk to see how the man who had put this fiasco together was taking it. All he saw was an empty chair. Edmunds had gone. Casually, Herbie got up and drifted out to the front of the building. Apart from the hum of traffic from the nearby road, everything was quiet. He moved over to the artist's car parking area. For a moment he heard nothing. Then the sound of metal on tarmac accompanied by a lot of angry puffing and blowing floated towards him on the night air. Edmunds was changing a tyre.

I was right, Herbie thought, he is trying to do a runner. I've got him nailed. All I have to do is to fleece him for the money, pay Amos the minimum and Edmunds can go fly a kite. I'd have well over £2,000 and no questions asked. A smattering of applause and one or two shouts of derision echoed faintly from inside the hall. So Amos was still up there, fighting the good fight. It was in its own way heroic. Then he remembered what it had cost Amos emotionally to do this gig. And those film students, played for suckers just because they were trying to do something creative. No, he couldn't do it, he had had it done to him too many times in the past. Everyone was going to get paid, the sound man, the lighting man, the film crew and the musicians, especially the musicians - everybody except one man.

Herbie stepped quietly forward and popped his head round the side of a van.

"Hello, Edmund, somebody let your tyre down? What a bummer."

CHAPTER 10
THE PARTY

"Hello, Bob - Herbie" He tossed a rolled cigarette into the air, tried to catch it with his mouth and failed. Bending down to retrieve it he dropped the receiver. He picked them both up.

"Of course I'm not drunk, I dropped the phone. Listen, are you doing anything with the van on Saturday, I've bought a juke box and I want to take it down to Cyn."

"It's a natch. So you're coming to the party."

"No, I promised this for last Christmas and I finally managed to get one. What party?"

There was a pause.

"I dunno, somebody mentioned something about something, probably nothing. Better give her a buzz in case she's going to be out, or sick, that's it, I think I heard that she's gonna be... I mean she is ill."

"What party?"

"Party? Who said anything about a party? I said so you're becoming arty, you know, the juke box."

Herbie clutched the receiver as if it was Bob's neck, but he managed to keep his voice quietly measured.

"The juke box is for Cyn, not for me and you didn't say arty you said party."

There was another pause.

"I'm sorry, mate, but maybe she doesn't want you to know."

"Well I do know. You can trust me, I don't want to go anywhere I'm not wanted."

"OK, Cyn's having a party on Saturday."

"And..."

"And nothing. That's it. She wants me to do the music, put some kind of Dixieland band together. I didn't like to mention money because, as you know, we go way back, but these guys will want paying, so I hope she comes through."

"Yeah, well, thanks for telling me. I'll see you later."

'Right, mate, we can do the juke box next week. Oh, I think she might have said something about it being an engagement party."

"What? Hey, Bob..." But the line had gone dead.

Herbie slowly replaced the receiver and slumped on to the settee. So Cynthia was getting married again, at least that would end the alimony payments. Why hadn't she told him? He had spoken to her only a week ago and she had only talked about the children - and about the money he owed her, but even then she hadn't complained, in fact, she had been surprisingly reasonable. Too reasonable. Of course, she had known that she soon would be getting rid of him forever. That was it, end of story. It was none of his business anyway. Whistling nonchalantly to himself, he got up to carry on with what he had been doing, but after walking round the flat a couple of times he couldn't remember what it was, so he went out and got drunk.

The next morning was sunny with a bright blue September sky which meant that Herbie was wearing sunglasses as he navigated the Volvo into Bell Street, Marylebone. He pulled up near a second hand clothes shop with an ancient mannequin in a dinner jacket standing outside and went in. He took the sunglasses off cautiously and allowed his eyes to adjust to the gloom. Gradually he became aware of a long, dark, musty room with lines of clothes on hangers taking up most of the available space. At the far end was a full length mirror with a small desk beside it. Above the desk was a parrot in a cage and behind it a man. On moving closer Herbie could see that he had the haughtily sensitive face of someone who might once have been an actor.

Silent and brooding, he seemed lost in thought, as if remembering past triumphs in theatres long closed. As he continued to sit there without moving, Herbie began to wonder if he was aware of his presence. Then a hand reached out, picked up a folded card and stood it on the corner of the desk facing towards him, it said, 'Thieves will be Prosecuted'.

"Good evening."

"Close, but no cigar," said Herbie. "Good morning."

"I didn't say anything," said the man, "please address your witticisms to the parrot."

"My mistake, "said Herbie, "is that all he says?"

"No, he also says good morning, but only in the afternoons."

"Quite a double act. I want a suit and a hat, something bright and theatrical, with plenty of razzmatazz."

"You in the business?"

"Entertainment? Yeah, that's it, the glare of the footlights." He attempted a rough impression of a dance step. The man moved the sign back to the other side of the desk and stood up.

"I've got one suit," he said, "it wouldn't be everybody's cup of tea. Do you remember the Black and White Minstrels, Sunday Night at the Palladium?"

"Yeah...er, vaguely," said Herbie.

"It's one of theirs, a real privilege to own, they were practically a theatrical tradition." He pushed aside a line of suits and reached down a white evening jacket and a pair of trousers with a stripe containing a myriad glittering sparkles down each leg. "Here it is," he said.

"I'll take it," said Herbie, "one more thing, where can I get a beard?"

As the taxi driver pulled through the gateposts with no gate and up the drive to the farm house that had once been his home, Dixieland Jazz drifted through the night air. Typical, thought Herbie, no one ever thinks of their own, that's a gig I could have done, no problem.

"I knew you were going to a party the minute I saw you," said the cab driver, gliding to a halt.

"Well done," said Herbie, "I suppose you learn to keep your eyes open in your game. How did you know I wasn't running away to join a circus?"

"Ha, Ha, very good, that'll be a tenner."

Herbie got out of the car and handed the driver a note.

"There you go, mate, sorry I haven't any change, be lucky."

He stepped quickly back, narrowly avoiding his foot being run over, as the taxi shook the dust from its wheels and burned for home. Turning he made his way round the side of the farm house to where the party was in full swing, the sound getting louder as he approached. But as he cleared the corner of the wall he stopped dead.

There were about a hundred people on his, as he still liked to think of it, front lawn. Tastefully lit by Chinese lanterns which crisscrossed above them, they were talking, drinking, smoking and even dancing, but what they weren't doing was wearing anything faintly resembling a white top hat and tails with pink stripes encrusted with glistening stars. The dress code was as casual as a trip to the supermarket.

Herbie scratched his itching beard and pondered. There was no staying incognito in that crowd. For some reason he had expected fancy dress, or at least an attempt to give a sense of occasion. In either case he could have got away with it, but amongst this lot he would look as if he had just tap danced his way out of a Busby Berkeley parade. Cyn's radar would home in and he wouldn't last five seconds. Then he saw the band.

On a makeshift stage under a canvas awning a motley collection of ageing jazzers in crumpled dinner jackets and bow ties were going through the motions. At the piano Bob was wearing a gold lame jacket that he had bought as a souvenir from Graceland and a straw hat. Compared to the audience they looked as bizarre as a collection of Tibetan monks on a spree, but this was show business, so no one was taking any notice of them.

That was the place, thought Herbie, up there he would fade into the background, yet still be able to keep an eye on what was going on. But how to get there? He had an old tenor banjo in the attic upstairs, but sure as hell there would be a string missing. No, he had to find a way to change places with someone on the stand. His piercing gaze homed in on the banjo player. He was a thick set, red faced man with grey, curly hair sitting on the far side of the stage from Bob near the front. Jammed into his shirt and jacket and with a neck that no bow tie would ever sit comfortably on, he was working like a demon, although, with the rest of the band crashing away, not much sound was coming through. Perfect, thought Herbie, whose tenor banjo skills were slightly rusty, now, how do I get him off stage?

He knew that quite often in these long gigs the band members would take a break one at a time to have a quick cigarette or a drink and, with the minor contribution he was making, the first was almost certain to be the banjo player. He decided to go backstage and wait for an opportunity to present itself. Striding confidently over to the bandstand, he tipped his hat to Bob, receiving a blank stare in return, and took up his post behind the canvas.

He didn't have long to wait. The sound changed and a few seconds later a tall, thin supercilious looking man pushed his way through a slit in the backdrop and stood beside him. He had been wrong, it was the clarinet player.

"What a great sound," said Herbie.

The clarinet player eyed him stonily while extracting a cigarette from a cigarette case and lighting up.

"Magician?" he asked, disinterestedly.

"It has been said," replied Herbie, "but I'm in your game."

"You playing to night?"

"That's what I want to talk to you about, I have to get on the stage, I'll explain later, but I've got to see what's going on."

"I can tell you what is going on, a whole lot of nothing. I nailed the Johnny Dodds solo in 'High Society' to not so much as a raised eyebrow. Do you play tuba?"

"No."

"Pity, this band could do with a bit more at the bottom end. Well, I'd better be getting back."

And before Herbie could say anything else he was gone.

Two more numbers went by and no one appeared backstage. Herbie began to fidget, time was passing and for all the good he was doing where he was he might as well have been at home. He walked round to the side of the stage, winked meaningfully at Bob and pointed to the rear. No reaction, just another blank stare, then he remembered the beard. Of course, Bob probably thought he was some nut from among the guests. He retreated once more to the back and took an exasperated pull on his rum flask.

Another few minutes went by in which he thought he heard St Louis Blues for the second time, then the sound changed again. This time it did seem as if some of the rhythm had dropped out. After a confused scratching on the canvas and a lot of puffing and blowing the banjo player emerged into the open.

"What a great sound," said Herbie.

"Yeah?" The banjo player pulled a half smoked cigar from his dinner jacket and started patting his pockets in search of a match. Herbie's lighter flared under his nose.

"Cheers. So you like that old rubbish, do you?"

"Couldn't sound any better if that was Eddie Condon up there instead of you."

"Needs a decent mic on it, and I should be much further up in the mix."

"You're so right. Can I offer you a drop of rum?"

"I wouldn't say no."

Herbie handed him the flask.

"Mud in your eye." The banjo player took a long swallow and passed it back. "A life saver. Nobody said anything about a magician, what time are you supposed to go on?"

"That is what I want to talk to you about. There has been a bit of a mix up. My name's John Hawkes, I'm a private detective. This is an expensive crowd, but there are always going to be one or two gate crashers. Mrs Watson can't afford to have anything go wrong, so they hired me to take care of things. Unfortunately, the girl at the office told me it was fancy dress."

"Ha, Ha, talk about incognito, you'll look like a right berk amongst that lot."

"Exactly, you've got it in one. Have you ever worked undercover?"

"No."

"You surprise me, have another drink."

"Maybe a small one. I've got to be getting back."

"Fifty quid."

"Pardon?"

"I'll give you fifty quid if you will let me take your place on the stand for half an hour."

"Sorry, the band leader wouldn't like it, I might lose my fee."

"Bob Harwood? He won't mind once he knows the situation, he's a friend of mine."

"But can you play the tenor banjo."

"Play it? Are you kidding? I used to do the river boats."

"Really? I wouldn't have said you were that old."

"Not the Mississippi, the Thames, they sometimes hire bands out for parties on weekends. Listen, we're wasting time, crimes may be being committed even as we speak. Here, take the money. Don't worry, it's nothing to me, it all goes on the bill."

"Well, I ..."

"And hang on to the rum flask, it might get in my way." Herbie handed it to him and disappeared through the slit in the canvas only for his head and arm to reappear a moment later. "Give us a loan of your pick will you?" The banjo player handed it to him and he was gone.

Nobody in the audience seemed to notice that a man in a black dinner jacket had left for a break and a man in a white top hat and tails had returned; and such was Herbie's manner that even the band accepted it with no more than a raised eyebrow.

"What's next?" he asked the clarinet player.

"St. Louis Blues again, in Bb."

They went into the number and, once Herbie had remembered where Bb was on the tenor banjo, he began to study the audience. Things had livened up a bit while he had been getting on stage. The conversation and laughter had got louder and more people were dancing. To his chagrin, he recognized quite a few of the guests. Brad Brainstorm was there, Big John Tucker and even Lorine. And who was paying for it? He was, or he would have been if his alimony payments had been up to date.

He looked around for Cyn. There she was, radiant in a high collared black dress with a silver spray on her breast, contrasting beautifully with her fair hair and pale complexion. She seemed happy and relaxed. Lorine strolled over and they started talking. Soon they were laughing away together and Herbie began to feel uncomfortable. What were they saying? He knew they had known each other in the old days, but he didn't know they were still in contact. He had seen Lorine off to the States soon after their last meeting, yet here she was back again. And she had not contacted him. What was going on? Well if they were discussing him he certainly wasn't getting the reverential treatment he would have hoped for. Cyn was fairly discreet but Lorine being a spacey California girl might say anything under the assumption that it was good therapy for someone, usually herself.

As the band went into Tiger Rag he began to feel like a deeply wronged man, not least because he was having a devil of a job keeping up with the chord changes. He'd forgotten that Bob could actually play the piano if he tried and right now he was trying to be Jelly Roll Morton. After a while things simmered down and Bob called a waltz. Herbie went broodingly back to watching the crowd.

Brad was practicing his person to person skills on a meaty, bull like man in a khaki shirt worn outside his shorts. He was pointing every now and then to Big John, who was standing nearby and, judging by the modest expression on Big John's face, he was laying it on with a trowel. Brad could never stop being an agent, he would have hired his mother out if there had been a knitting circuit. Suddenly, Big John looked up and saw Cynthia standing alone a few yards away. He walked over, took her hand and said something in her ear. She smiled and nodded. Then he saw some one congratulating him and clapping him on the back. Big John thanked him while Cynthia looked on admiringly.

A blinding flash illuminated Herbie's brain, everything became crystal clear. She was going to marry Big John. Of course, he had been over quite a lot during the summer, Brad had introduced them and this was the result. And not one of them had even had the courtesy to send him a post card. To think of Cynthia marrying a great lumbering lug like that, a man who knew zip about playing the blues.

The clarinet played a mocking solo. Herbie's head was spinning. Big John and Cynthia walked over towards the bandstand, he took her in his arms and they started to dance. They were closer now and Herbie could hear what Big John, never the quietest man on the planet, was saying.

"Hey, you sure are a cute little thing. I'm gonna enjoy gettin' to know you better."

These were the last words he was to utter for some time because, as he finished speaking, a banjo, swung in a wide arc, descended from the bandstand and crashed into the back of his head. Big John crumpled to the ground, Cynthia screamed and Bob leapt to his feet, cutting the band with a gesture.

"Herbie!" he yelled.

The next second the man in the khaki shirt had yanked him from the stage. The fall jerked him free and he fell over. Springing to his feet, he readjusted his hold on the banjo and was leaning back to give himself a full swing at his attacker when two more men grabbed him by the arms. The banjo slipped from his grasp and hit the earth with a jarring discord.

"You crazy loon, what was that all about? You might have killed him." The man in kaki was shaking with anger and it was obvious that the only thing stopping him from taking Herbie apart was the fact that he was already being held by two men.

"No bastard is going to marry my wife without a fight," muttered Herbie doggedly.

Cynthia, who had rolled Big John over on to his side in the recovery position, looked up when she heard his voice.

"Oh, no, I might have known it would be you," she said, "who told you I was marrying Big John?"

Before he could reply, Lorine, sobbing distractedly, rushed up with a jug of water and a handkerchief and began bathing the blood and matted hair at the back of Big John's head. For a minute, nothing could be heard except the sound of dripping water and Lorine snuffling through her tears, then there was a low groan.

"Johnny, oh Johnny, are you hurt, honey," cried Lorine.

Big John opened one eye and squinted up at her for a moment, then, with superb restraint, he decided not to answer the question and move right along.

"What happened?" he asked.

Herbie looked down and saw five foot two of very angry Cynthia looking up at him.

"It's all right she said to the two men, "you can let him go, he won't cause any more trouble, he is my ex" (heavy emphasis on the ex) "husband."

The two men let him go and Herbie, feeling like a man who had spoken too loudly in a quiet restaurant, moved a few paces away. Cynthia followed him.

"Who told you," she repeated in a tense whisper, "that I was going to marry Big John?"

"Bob said it was an engagement party."

"It is an engagement party - for Lorine and Big John. She thought it wouldn't be tactful to invite you."

Herbie saw daylight. A wave of joy washed over him, then the enormity of what he had done hit him. He had nearly killed somebody and ruined the party into the bargain. What could he do? Never a man to dodge the unavoidable, he decided to face up to it.

"Sorry, Cyn, I got my wires crossed. Half a mo'."

He dashed round to the back of the stage where the banjo player, completely oblivious to the chaos out front, was sitting quietly on the grass sipping from the flask.

"Emergency," said Herbie, grabbing it from him and taking it over to Big John who was now sitting in a chair.

"I know you don't drink," he said, "but this is me-dicinal, have a good slug."

Big John, who had been teetotal for five long years, immediately saw the wisdom in Herbie's remark. It was true, it was medicine, even Lorine wouldn't object. He accepted the proffered flask and took two generous mouthfuls. He felt the spirit seeping into him, spreading a warm friendly glow. The thumping in his head began to recede, his eyes cleared to a sharper focus. He gazed dreamily at the flask in his hand for a long moment, then he screwed the top on and handed it back.

As Herbie put the flask away he noticed that all eyes were upon him and he instinctively knew that he was not the most popular man in the garden. It was up to him to do something to put the evening back on an even keel, but what was it? For a moment nothing occurred to him, then he had it, he must apologize.

"John," he said, "I've got to admit I was totally out of order, what can I say? Will you accept my apologies?"

A much revived Big John climbed to his feet'

"Herbie," he replied, "I will, if you can accept my apologies for this." His huge fist, swung low from the ground, caught Herbie perfectly on the chin and sent him arching backwards to fall insensible about six yards away.

"Yeehaa!" A piercing yell from Brad rent the air. "Wow!" he said, "what a great party, it's just like a John Wayne movie."

"At least they're polite about it," said Bob, "come on, someone help me get him inside.

When Herbie came to he was lying on the couch in the sitting room. There was a lamp on in one corner, the rest of the room was in shadow. He felt his jaw gingerly trying to convince himself it was still hinged on correctly, then he saw Cynthia sitting quietly at the end of the couch watching him. He struggled to a sitting position and gave her a lopsided grin. They were silent for a moment.

"Everything all right," he said, at last.

"Seems to be. I think they are enjoying themselves even more. Attempted murder tends to loosen the atmosphere at a party.

"You know it wasn't that, Cyn, I lost my head."

"But why?"

"I..." he paused, "I don't know."

Cynthia was looking at him strangely, he saw that one hand was clutching a screwed up handkerchief and he realized that she must have been crying before he had woken up.

"I've made a pigs ear of things, haven't I?" he said.

"Lancelot wasn't perfect."

"No."

"But that did not stop him fighting for someone he loved."

"Yeah, I love old Chaucer."

"Mallory."

"Of course, what was I thinking about?" He stood up. "Well, I'd better make myself scarce."

"I don't think you're fit to travel."

He paused and their eyes met.

"You're right," he said, "I could do with a lie down. Come and tell me when the guests have gone."

"I will," she said, "and for God's sake get rid of that beard."

ABOUT THE AUTHOR

James Flynn is a songwriter, singer and guitarist. He is married and lives in London.

www.ingramcontent.com/pod-product-compliance
Lightning Source LLC
Chambersburg PA
CBHW071519170626
46811CB00007B/2903